First published 2011 by
A & C Black Publishers Ltd
36 Soho Square, London, W1D 3QY

www.acblack.com

Text copyright © 2011 Jenny Alexander
Illustrations copyright © 2011 Ella Okstad

ISBN 978-1-4081-3287-6
A CIP catalogue for this book is available from the British Library.

Printed and bound in Great Britain
by TJ International Ltd, Cornwall.

JENNY ALEXANDER

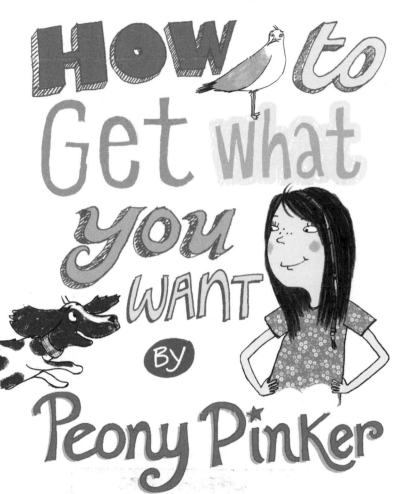

How to Get what you WANT By Peony Pinker

A & C Black • London

Contents

Chapter 1

The Jack Russell and the Pit Bulls

You know when something bad keeps happening such as, for example, your big sister, Primrose, brings her horrible new best friend home every single day after school?

And you've got no reason to suppose that today will be any different but you just can't help hoping that, by some kind of magic, it might be?

And then you get home and there they are — Primrose rummaging in the cupboards for something to eat and Bianca, sitting on the kitchen table swinging her feet... and your heart sinks into your boots.

Well, that's what happened to me the day I decided enough was enough.

'Look who's here,' said Bianca, as soon as I walked in the door. Primrose didn't bother to look. She went on rummaging. I felt as welcome as a slug in a welly.

I was hungry myself but I couldn't get a snack or Bianca would call me Peony Podge and say I looked like a walrus. I saw a walrus on David Attenborough the other night and it looked like a big bag of blubber.

Bianca swung her stick-thin legs. Her school skirt was nearly up to her knickers. I don't know how she gets away with it. I don't know how she gets away with wearing so much make-up either, or that red stripe in her hair. She pulled her pony-tail tighter.

'What are you staring at, Pea-brain?' she snapped. She's got lots of names for me and none of them are nice.

I went upstairs. The kitchen takes up the whole of the ground floor of our house, and the sitting room takes up the whole of the floor above. Then there's my bedroom and Primrose's above that and finally

Mum and Dad's bedroom and his study in the attic. All the houses in Harbour Row are very tall and thin.

I chucked my bag in the nearest armchair, grabbed the remote and flung myself down on the settee. With any luck, Primrose and Bianca would stay downstairs. They couldn't go out because Primrose was supposed to be looking after me until Mum or Dad got home from work.

Five measly minutes, that's all I got, and then they came crashing up the stairs.

'Bye-bye, Peony Pudding!'

Bianca yanked the cushion out from behind my back.

'We're going to play Disco Divaz.'

Primrose snatched the remote and switched on the PlayStation.

'But I'm watching the Dog Whisperer.'

'Tough,' said Primrose. 'There's two of us and only one of you.'

It obviously wasn't fair because Bianca didn't live in our house so she shouldn't count, but when I said so before it just made things fifty billion times worse. No exaggeration.

I went upstairs. Primrose's bedroom door was shut. I walked into my own room, closed the door and sat down on the edge of the bed.

Boom badda boom badda boom badda boom badda boom... The backing track kicked in and then Primrose and Bianca started screeching into their microphones like a couple of strangled cats in the room below.

Surely Primrose couldn't seriously think they had any chance of becoming pop stars? But you never knew. Since she had started hanging out with Bianca she hadn't just turned nasty – she had turned stupid too.

I tried to block out the noise by reading my new library book, Incredible Dogs. It was full of true stories about, well, incredible dogs. True Story Number One was called 'George, a Little Hero with a Great Big Heart'. It was about this nine-year-old Jack Russell terrier who was out for a walk with some children when a pair of Pit Bulls suddenly attacked them.

The Pit Bulls went for the smallest child, who was only four, and they would have killed him if George hadn't dived in to defend him. The Pit Bulls let go of the child and turned on George instead. He didn't have a chance. But through his incredible courage he saved the children, even though it cost him his life. The people in the town where he lived put up a statue of George to honour him and he was awarded the highest medal an animal can get for bravery.

I've always thought that if I was a dog I would be a Jack Russell terrier. 'Bold and friendly', it says they are in The Bumper Book of Dogs. Also 'intelligent and brave'. That might sound big-headed but I'm obviously not going to choose a breed that's supposed to be 'wimpy and dim'! Mentioning no names, in case you've got one.

Boom badda boom badda boom badda boom badda boom... The noise was so loud it was making the house shake. Three pencils rattled across my desk and threw themselves on the floor in despair. I didn't want to spoil the rest of the stories by trying to read them with bad singing battering my eardrums.

Picking up the pencils gave me an idea. I made a poster that said:

Big sister, age 15. Free to good home.

Underneath, I did a picture of Primrose.

When I had finished I sat back to admire it. Then I crossed out 'good home' and wrote 'anyone who will have her' instead. It felt good imagining someone coming to fetch her and take her away. But the good feeling didn't last because just then, Primrose and Bianca moved on from raps to power ballads.

No-one should have to hear my big sister Primrose and her horrible new best friend sing power ballads. I put my hands over my ears. The only way out of the house was back down through the sitting room. I didn't want to go past them again, but I couldn't stand it. I was in agony! Seriously, the police could use Primrose and Bianca to force confessions out of people. 'Own up, or they do Endless Love…'

I crept down the stairs and tried to slip past without them noticing but they stopped singing and pressed Pause. They glared at me.

'Stop spying on us, Pea-brain,' said Bianca.

'I'm not spying on you. I'm not even interested in you!'

'Ooh!' They raised their eyebrows at each other. They mimicked me. 'I'm-not-even-interested!'

Then they laughed and Bianca said, 'I don't like you hanging around us all the time, and Primrose doesn't like it either.'

As if it was possible to avoid them in number 13, Harbour Row.

'Neither does Annabel!' added Primrose.

They both snorted with laughter. There was nobody except us three in the room. I couldn't help myself.

'Who's Annabel?'

'That's for us to know and you to find out,' said Bianca. 'Now go away and leave us in peace.'

Peace! That was rich. I trudged on down to the kitchen. The noise started up again. The back door was blocked by a half-dead cheese-plant and anyway there wasn't anything out that way except the yard. The garden of our house got sold off years ago, before we even moved here. Now Mr Kaminski next door's got a big L-shaped garden he never uses and we've got the bit by the back door that hardly gets any sunshine.

I went out the front door, pulled it shut behind me and sat down on the top step in the sun. I found myself thinking about the story of George and I wondered, could I be as gutsy as him? If I was George, then my Pit Bulls would be Bianca and Primrose. They were much bigger than me, they were meaner, and also it was two against one.

The problem was, I had no more chance against Primrose and Bianca than George had against the Pit Bulls. You can be as brave as you like, but let's face it, if you're small you won't win on your own.

I would never normally tell tales — ask anyone. I didn't tell the day Primrose bunked off school or the time I saw her and Bianca smoking at the beach. But enough was enough. Something had to be done.

Chapter 2
The saviour of the sick and the accidental agony aunt

'Hello, Peony!'

Mum didn't come straight up but hung her bag on the railing and started hauling the wheelbarrow out from the storage space under the front steps. I didn't answer, so then she had to look at me properly.

'Everything all right?' she asked. But before I had a

chance to answer, she said, 'I won't be two ticks,' and trundled the wheelbarrow back up the hill. I hate it when she does that.

The houses in this part of Polgotherick were built before anyone had cars, on steep zig-zag pathways that go all the way down to the harbour. You have to park on the road at the top and walk down, and if you need to bring something big from the car you have to go back up and fetch it in your wheelbarrow.

Quite a lot more than two ticks later, Mum came back. She parked the wheelbarrow at the bottom of the steps and wiped the sweat off her forehead. There was a huge plant in it that looked like a load of outsize tulip leaves tightly crammed into a bucket. The tips of the leaves were mostly brown or missing.

'Can you give me a hand with this aspidistra?'

It was hard to get hold of the pot underneath all the leaves and when we did, it weighed a ton, so after the first few steps we had to put it down and have a rest. Mum stood on the step below, stopping the pot from toppling with her foot. It seemed like the perfect time to tell her about Primrose and Bianca. If she tried to take off in the middle of me talking, the aspidistra would be a goner.

'Mum,' I said. 'Primrose and Bianca are being horrible to me.'

They had turned the music down, just like they always did when Mum was about to get home. And they said I was a suck-up!

Mum sighed.

'You and Primrose have always had your ups and downs,' she said.

'This isn't ups and downs. For one thing, there aren't any ups any more. She never watches Neighbours with me or helps me with my homework or tells me about her day. She's horrible all the time.'

Mum bent down to pick up the aspidistra again but I didn't move. She glanced up at me. I crossed my arms over my chest so she could see that I wasn't going anywhere until she listened to me.

'OK, I'll have a word with Primrose,' she said. 'Now can we shift this aspidistra, please?'

I still didn't budge.

'Tell her she can't have Bianca round after school any more.'

Mum's face lit up as if a light-bulb had gone on inside her head.

'Oh, I see what this is all about,' she said. 'You're feeling left out. I know Primrose can be a bit full-on when she has a new best friend, but things will soon settle down.'

She nodded towards the aspidistra as if to say,

'Now can we move it?' But I looked straight past her at the sparkling sea and the boats bobbing way down in the harbour. They looked like toy boats in a big blue bath.

Mum took a deep breath. It was the one that means, 'I'm not annoyed right now but I will be very soon.'

'I'm not going to tell Primrose that she can't have her friends over after school, Peony. You wouldn't like it if I said you couldn't have your friends over, would you?'

'My friends are nice,' I said. 'They aren't mean and nasty like Bianca.'

'I don't know why you've got such a bee in your bonnet about Bianca,' said Mum. 'She seems fine to me and she's certainly cheered Primrose up.'

I couldn't argue with that. Before Bianca came along, Primrose had been in a moochy mood for nearly a month because her boyfriend Marcus had dumped her. She holed herself up in her room every day after school and only came down for supper, when she just sat there pushing her food around the plate as if it was a scientific specimen that had turned out to be not very interesting.

Mum and Dad were really worried. I was sure one of the reasons they both liked Bianca was that they were grateful to her for getting Primrose out of her mega-mooch.

Mum bent down and picked up her side of the pot in a that's-enough-now kind of way. We wrestled the aspidistra up the last few steps and put it down just inside the door.

'Hmm... where are we going to put it?' she said, scratching her head.

The big window at the front was already crammed with sick plants she had brought home from the Green Fingers Garden Centre because she couldn't bear to throw them away when her boss told her to. The windows and the glass door at the back were full of plants too. All they needed was a bit of TLC, she said. That's tender loving care. *Well*, I was thinking, *what about some TLC for me?*

We heard Primrose and Bianca coming down the stairs. They came into the kitchen wearing bikini tops and shorts, with beach towels under their arms. Primrose had never bothered about the beach before, but she and Bianca had started going down there most days recently. They probably thought they were so good looking they might get spotted by a talent scout or something.

'Hello, Mrs P,' Bianca said, all sweetness and light. 'Would you like me and Primrose to move that plant out to the yard for you before we go to the beach?'

'No, that's OK, Bianca,' said Mum. 'I haven't really decided where I'm going to put it yet and anyway, Peony's here so she can give me a hand.'

Primrose and Bianca sauntered off down to the beach. I wished I had special powers so I could zap them with hate-rays and send them rolling down the zig-zag paths all the way to the sea. Crash, splash, gurgle - gone!

'Let's have a cup of tea while we're thinking about it,' said Mum. I wished she had special powers so she could read my thoughts. If she could see that what I was thinking she might take a bit more notice.

As the kettle was reaching the boil, Dad got home. He crashed straight into the aspidistra.

'For crying out loud, Jan!' he grumbled, squeezing past. He put his laptop down on the table and flopped down on the nearest chair. You didn't need to be Sherlock Holmes to see he was having a difficult day.

'You won't believe what Ed wants me to do now.'

'Table tennis?' asked Mum. 'Tiddly-winks?'

Dad's a sports reporter on the Three Towns Gazette. Ed is his editor. I always thought it was short for Edward but come to think of it, maybe it's actually short for 'editor'.

'Daphne's gone missing and that means we haven't

got an agony aunt, so Ed wants me to take over until he's managed to track her down.'

'You!' gasped Mum. 'An agony aunt?'

'Well, exactly,' said Dad. 'He says I haven't got much work now the football season's over so I can do it in my spare time. Which is hardly the point. I mean, just look at these.'

He unzipped the front of his laptop case, took out a bundle of letters and emails and slapped them down on the table.

'How am I supposed to know what to say to Worried of Trethornden, who thinks the reason her husband left her is because she's got wobbly thighs? I haven't even seen her thighs!'

Mum shook her head. 'I really don't think you should agree to do this,' she said. 'Tell Ed you can't.'

'That's what I did. "I can't do it," I said. But he said, "Yes you can, and you're going to, unless you want to lose that cushy sports reporting job." He reckons everyone else in the office is too busy.'

Dad sifted through the letters, reading bits out.

'"Dear Daphne, I'm scared of doorknobs... Dear Daphne, Next door's cat treats my garden like a toilet... Dear Daphne..."' He stopped reading. 'I'm Daphne,' he groaned, 'and these people think *they've* got problems!'

Now normally I wouldn't have even tried to talk to Dad about stuff like Primrose being horrible but under the circumstances, with him suddenly being an agony aunt and all, I thought it might be worth a try.

'Dad,' I said. 'Primrose is being really horrible to me, not just normal horrible. And it's all the time too, not just when she's in a mood.'

He blinked as if I had asked him to grow wings and have a fly around.

'What do you want me to do about it?' he asked.

'Well, give me some advice,' I said. 'After all, you are an agony aunt, and that's what agony aunts are supposed to do.'

Dad looked at Mum. She shrugged.

'I think Peony's just feeling a bit left out because Primrose is spending so much time with Bianca,' she said. 'We all know how full-on Primrose can be when she's got a new friend. It'll soon settle down.'

'There you are then,' said Dad. 'It'll soon settle down. No need to get your knickers in a knot.'

So that was that. Anyone would think a saviour of the sick – even if it's just sick plants – and an agony aunt – even an accidental one like Dad – could come up with something a bit more caring than 'Don't get your knickers in a knot.'

Mum poured out the tea and opened a new packet

of custard creams. Trying not to think about that walrus on David Attenborough, I took two and went upstairs to watch Neighbours.

If you aren't naturally a snitch it can be tough when you work yourself up to tell on your big sister and nobody takes it seriously.

Chapter 3

Better in the morning...
worse than ever in the
afternoon

One of Dad's favourite mottos is 'Everything will look better in the morning.'

Mum says that's probably because he's too lazy to deal with anything today. But on this occasion he was right because the next morning was Saturday, and Saturday was always the best day of the week.

The alarm went off at half past six and I was out of the house by seven. When I first started helping at the kennels Mum used to get up and have breakfast with me but now she just came down all bleary-eyed to see me off when I was ready to leave. I didn't mind. I liked the feeling of being the only one awake in the house while everyone else was sleeping.

I walked up the zig-zag path in the early morning sunshine. There was a layer of mist out to sea but you could tell the sun would burn it off because the air was already really warm.

I came out onto the top road and crossed into Pentilly Close. Becky, the other Saturday helper, was waiting for me outside her house. She was wearing her usual cut-off jeans and tee-shirt. Her spiky black hair was still wet from the shower.

All the bungalows in Pentilly Close had big back gardens and in the far corner of Becky's there was a summer house. It had a square of faded carpet on the floor and a big squashy settee, and when you went in it smelt dry and warm, like old sunshine. Becky was so lucky. If I had a summer house like that I could go out to it every day after school. I could take some snacks and do my homework in peace. I could pretend Primrose and Bianca never existed.

The kennels were in Hayden's Lane so we went

to the end of the close and took the footpath across the field. Becky knew all about Primrose and Bianca because I had told her one day when I was feeling fed up. She was thirteen, but she never talked down to me. It had been partly her idea that I should try telling Mum and Dad.

'I tried to tell them yesterday,' I said. 'But they wouldn't listen.'

'What did they say?'

'They think I'm jealous of Bianca because Primrose hasn't got time for me now she's round our house every day.'

Becky pulled a piece of grass and started chewing on it as we walked along. There were bees buzzing in the hedge and little birds flitting between the branches.

'I think you should try again,' she said.

'What's the point?'

'Well, if they think you're just jealous you probably didn't explain it well enough. You need to make them understand what's going on and how fed up you feel.'

It seemed to me that I had been really clear. I'd said exactly what was going on. They should have understood. They simply didn't want to.

'OK,' said Becky, 'then could you just have chosen the wrong time?'

I groaned. Yes, that was it! How could I have been so stupid? Of course Mum wouldn't listen when she was trying to work out what to do with a sick aspidistra. Of course Dad wouldn't listen when he was struggling with the stress of suddenly being Daphne.

We climbed over the stile into Hayden's Lane.

'It's Lollie's last day today,' Becky said, changing the subject.

Lollie was a bouncy black spaniel that had been at the kennels for three weeks. Her name was short for Lollipop, but Becky and me said it should be long for lol, because 'laugh out loud' was what she made us do.

Some dogs when they first came in were nose-under-the-paw anxious and sad. Some were aggressive and tried to run away. But Lollie was happy-go-lucky. She settled straight in.

'At least her owner isn't coming till this afternoon,' Becky said. 'We'll be able to play with her one last time after we've finished.'

We met Matt coming down the lane. He was on his way to work. Now he was seventeen he had a proper summer job that paid more money than he used to get working for his parents at the kennels.

My mum had got talking to his mum at the Easter parade.

26

His mum: 'Matt's going to be working week-ends at the Crocodile Cafe so we'll be short-handed at the kennels this summer.'

My mum: 'I know Peony's only young but I'm sure she'd love to help out if you'd be willing to give her a try.'

Way to go, Mum!

My mum knows Becky's mum too because they were in the same class at school, so she also fixed up for me and Becky to walk to the kennels together. Obviously, I wasn't that keen at first, what with Becky being so much older than me, but it turned out to be brilliant because she's animal-mad like me and really nice.

Matt grinned at us. 'It's going to be a real scorcher today,' he said. 'Looks like we'll all be working with hot dogs!' We heard him chuckling at his own joke as he walked on down the lane.

We went to the barn first as usual to pick up our mops and buckets and see if there were any new arrivals. Each dog had a box in the barn with its name on and the number of the pen it was in. Inside the box there were things the owner had brought from home - enough food for the dog's stay, any medicines it needed, its lead and sometimes some favourite toys.

Matt's mum came out of the farmhouse waving four new packs of rubber gloves.

'I've got a lovely bunch of Marigolds!' she said.

All the Teversons had the same sense of humour. Matt's younger brother Jay was always making terrible jokes. Like, there were two fleas that needed to get home – one said to the other, 'Shall we walk or take the dog?' Say no more.

We filled our buckets from the outside tap and picked up our mops. Lollie barked a happy hello when she saw us in the yard so we went over to see her before we got stuck into mopping out the pens and walking the other dogs.

I was mostly only allowed to walk the smaller ones but I could walk a big one if it had a nice nature, such as Harold the Newfoundland who came in most weekends. The Bumper Book of Dogs calls Newfoundlands 'the gentle giants of the dog world'. That was Harold all right.

Becky mopped out Harold's pen while I walked him round the three meadows that belonged to the kennels, then I mopped out Dot the Dalmatian's while Becky took her for a walk, and so on all the way along our side of the yard. Mrs Teverson and Jay did the double pens and the dogs that had to be kept separate because if they so much as saw another dog they would go mental.

It was too hot to hurry so we took our time. We had lots of stops for cold drinks. There wasn't a breath of wind and the thunder flies were really bad out in the meadows. If Bianca and Primrose singing power ballads didn't work, the police could use thunder flies to make people talk.

We saved Lollie till last. I always used to walk her while Becky mopped out her pen and then we would both take her back out and throw her favourite toy for her, a rubber cupcake that squeaked when you squeezed it.

I put her on the lead and we set off round the meadows. We were half way round the farthest one when the sky suddenly went dark as if a giant silent spaceship had come over and was hovering right above us, blocking out the light. An eerie silence settled over everything, as if the birds and bees had stopped to listen.

Lollie and I stopped too. We stood there looking at each other for a few seconds. Then, just as we were about to start walking again, there was a flash of lightning and the loudest crack of thunder I had ever heard in my life. It was like a bomb going off. I dropped to the ground as if I'd been shot. Lollie gave an almighty heave on her lead, slipped her collar and threw herself under the hedge.

I felt one or two big drops of rain on my back, and then the skies opened. It was like a waterfall. I was drenched in seconds. I struggled to my feet, calling Lollie's name, but I could hardly hear my own voice above the racket of the rain.

I called and called, searching frantically along the bottom of the hedge, but Lollie didn't come. My clothes were stuck to my body, as cold and clammy as wet seaweed, and my trainers were full of water. Blinking the rain out of my eyes, I looked down at Lollie's empty lead in my hand. I had to run back to the kennels and get help.

The rain was bouncing off the baked earth, making sudden puddles all around. I splashed back along the path through the meadows, slipping and sliding as I went, almost falling over every time the thunder crashed overhead.

Everyone was sheltering in the barn.

'There you are!' cried Mrs Teverson. 'We were just about to send out a search party.'

'Where's Lollie?' said Becky.

'She slipped her lead! What are we going to do?'

I was shivering so hard I could hardly get the words out. Mrs Teverson put her arm round me.

'Don't worry,' she said. 'Lollie will be sheltering somewhere. She'll come out soon enough when the storm blows over. But right now, we'd better get you dry before you catch your death.'

We all ran across to the farmhouse, where Mrs Teverson gave me a towel and some dry clothes to put on. By the time I had got dry, the rain had stopped as suddenly as it began. The sun had come back out and steam was rising from the concrete in the yard.

I borrowed a dry pair of wellies, two sizes too big, and we went back outside to look for Lollie. The grass in the paddock was splashy under our feet. I showed them the place where Lollie had run under the hedge. But she wasn't there now. She was nowhere to be seen.

We called her name. We squeaked her rubber cupcake. Becky rattled the box of doggie chocs her owner had left for her. But Lollie didn't come.

Chapter 4
Homeward Bound and Dad's first 'Dear Daphne'

Mrs Teverson sent me and Becky home at the usual time though we wanted to stay and keep looking for Lollie.

'Your parents will be wondering where you've got to,' she said.

I told Dad what had happened over lunch. There was no-one else in the house. Primrose and Bianca were still at the beach. They must have taken shelter in the beach toilets or cafe until the storm had passed. Mum was at work.

According to Mum, the Green Fingers Garden Centre did brisk business on Saturdays. According to Dad, Accident and Emergency probably did brisk business on Sundays with all the people she had sold power mowers and hedge cutters to the day before.

'What if Lollie doesn't come back?' I said. 'What if her owner comes to collect her and she isn't there? What if Mrs Teverson doesn't want me to work at the kennels any more?'

'That's a lot of "what ifs",' said Dad. 'What if Lollie does come back? What if her owner finds her safe and well when he comes to pick her up? What if Mrs Teverson is perfectly happy with your work? It could happen!'

I felt as if he was palming me off because he didn't want to be bothered with my problems. But then he said, 'Why don't I phone Mrs T? I'll tell her how worried you are and see if she's got any news about Lollie.'

He put down his half-eaten sandwich and picked up the phone. I could hear his side of the conversation so I already knew before he told me that Lollie hadn't come back. 'But on the up-side,' Dad said, 'her owner hasn't shown up either yet so if she gets back soon he

33

might not even need to know she's been missing.'

Dad told me not to worry. 'Mrs T isn't worried. She says Lollie will come back when she's ready.'

I couldn't tell whether he was just saying that to cheer me up.

'She also says you're one of the best workers she's ever had and she's got no intention of letting you go.'

Yes, I thought, *he is just saying things to cheer me up*. Then I felt worse than ever.

Dad chomped through the rest of his sandwich. He followed it up with a banana and a slice of coffee cake. He seemed to be thinking hard about something, probably what to watch on the sports channel that afternoon.

'You know what we could do?' he said, suddenly perking up. 'We could watch that DVD you love. What's it called now? Homeward Bound!'

I gawped at him. He wasn't exactly a dog-lover ever since his best friend's German Shepherd bit him on the bum when he was nine. He'd certainly never shown the slightest interest in watching Homeward Bound with me, even though I had seen it seven times, three of them with Mum.

'Isn't it about dogs that find their way home?' he said. 'That sounds just the ticket under the circumstances.'

If you haven't seen Homeward Bound you should put it on your Christmas list right now. It's no good borrowing it because you're going to want to watch it again and again.

It's about a Bulldog called Chance, a Golden Retriever called Shadow and a sarcastic cat called Sassy. They get left with friends when their family go away, but they don't know what's going on so they try to find their way home. They get into all kinds of danger, and you keep feeling like your heart has stopped in your chest. Several times you think one of them has died and you simply can't stop yourself from crying.

I always cry. Dad cried too. He tried not to let me see, wiping his face on his sleeve, but then he gave up and got a box of tissues. As the final credits rolled he blew his nose and took a long deep breath.

To be honest, although it was nice watching Homeward Bound with Dad, it didn't exactly cheer me up. It got me thinking about all the dangers Lollie might be facing right now, out in the world all on her own. She wasn't a wise old dog like Shadow or a strong tough dog like Chance. She was as daft as a brush and as soft as butter.

It also got me thinking something that hadn't occurred to me before. What if Lollie was trying to find her way home, not to the kennels but to her real home? It was thirty miles away, across main roads, and Lollie had the road sense of a suicidal hedgehog.

'Feeling a bit better now?' asked Dad. I nodded. Well, I couldn't very well tell him his lovely idea had actually made me feel worse.

I didn't know what to do with myself after that. I just worried, worried, worried. I hovered by the phone. When Mum finally came home I told her what had happened while Dad was laying the table and she was unwrapping the fish and chips. She always gets something from the Castle Street chippie on her way home on Saturdays.

Primrose and Bianca came back from the beach just in time for tea.

'Have you been crying?' Primrose said, as soon as we all sat down.

I was going to say I'd just been watching a sad film, but Mum went and told her the whole story before I could stop her.

Bianca was all fake concern. 'How terrible for you,' she said. 'I mean, you must feel like it's all your fault. Well, I suppose it is your fault really.'

I glared at her. Mum said something about accidents happening.

'And dogs are always getting run over, aren't they?'

Bianca said. 'You must be so worried something bad could happen.'

Primrose mentioned a cat she had seen lying at the roadside that had been hit by a car but not killed. It was writhing in agony. Really dreadful, she said. Really upsetting.

'I'm sure Lollie will be all right,' Mum said, firmly. 'None of you must worry.' Surely she didn't think Primrose and Bianca actually cared!

After supper, they went back to the beach. I helped Mum to clear the dishes and then hung around while Dad showed her his ideas for his first ever problem page. He'd been working on it all morning and was feeling pleased with himself.

'It was quite easy once I got going,' he said, 'and I think I'm actually quite good at it!'

Mum wasn't so sure. She read some bits out loud.

Dear Daphne,

My girlfriend's fantastic in every way except she isn't into tennis and won't let me watch it on TV. With Wimbledon coming up, what can I do?

Frustrated Fan

Dear Frustrated Fan,

Your girlfriend sounds a bit bossy and she isn't going to change. There are plenty more fish in the sea, so I say ditch her and get a new girlfriend who shares your love of tennis.

Dad was nodding enthusiastically as Mum read. Mum looked doubtful. 'Is that the kind of advice Daphne usually gives?'

'Yes!' exclaimed Dad. 'She used the exact same expression last week to Heartbroken of Hillbrow, whose girlfriend walked out on him. There are plenty more fish in the sea, she said.'

'But that's different,' Mum pointed out. 'Heartbroken had already lost his girlfriend. Daphne was trying to cheer him up.'

Dad shrugged. The difference was lost on him. Mum moved on to the next problem.

Dear Daphne,

All my life I've wanted to be an opera singer but I just haven't had the breaks...

'Blah, blah...' Mum skimmed through the rest of the letter. Then she read Dad's answer.

Dear Sad Soprano,

It's good to have dreams. They stop you from dying of boredom at work and provide entertainment when there's nothing good on TV. But dreams don't always come true. What I say is, if you can't get what you want, get over it.

'If you can't get what you want, get over it' was another of Dad's favourite mottos along with, 'If at first you don't succeed, give up.'

The phone rang. It was Mrs Teverson. She wanted to speak to me. I was so nervous I nearly dropped the handset when Mum passed it over.

'Good news, Peony,' Mrs Teverson said. 'Lollie's back. I thought you'd like to know at once.'

I would have burst into tears of relief but I seemed to have used them all up blubbing through Homeward Bound.

'Her owner hasn't shown up yet so he doesn't even need to know that she's been missing,' Mrs Teverson went on. 'He probably said Sunday, not Saturday, and I just wrote it down wrong. I do hope this hasn't put you off working up here?'

I found my voice.

'No! No, of course not!'

'I'll see you next week, then.'

Mum and Dad were grinning at me. When I came off the phone Dad was all puffed up. 'What did I tell you?' he said. 'Lollie will probably come back – that's what I said – and her owner could well be delayed and not even know she's been missing and besides, whatever happens, Mrs T will definitely want you to go on helping at the kennels.'

He looked at Mum.

'That was good advice, wasn't it? See – I do know what I'm doing!'

'I didn't say your advice was bad,' Mum pointed out. 'Just that it might not be the kind of thing the real Daphne would say.'

'The real Daphne is missing,' Dad declared. 'No-one has any idea where she is. She is a person who hasn't even got the common sense to find her way into work or phone in sick if she can't make it. I, on the other hand, am a practical and down-to-earth person. My advice is full of common sense. It's a breath of fresh air after Daphne's airy-fairy wafflings and Ed is going to love it!'

Chapter 5
Choc-chip cookies and shoe-box beans

Sunday was a nice day. I didn't have to worry about Lollie any more, Dad was in a whistling mood because he'd decided that being Daphne wasn't going to be too hard after all, Mum only worked till lunch-time and, the icing on the cake, Primrose and Bianca spent the whole day at the beach.

Mum said, 'Why don't you ask a friend round?' but I like being on my own. Primrose says that makes me a Sad Loner. Just because she's a Sad Best-Friend-Addict.

Anyway, I took a stack of toast up to my bedroom and read the rest of the stories in my book about Amazing Dogs. Then I found some pictures of dogs on the internet and printed them off for my wall. That brought the number of breeds I had up to 37, all lined up in neat rows in the space between the door and the bookcase.

I lay down on my bed and looked at them, one by one. Just looking at them always made me feel happy. Feeling happy, I started to wonder whether Mum and Dad could be right. Perhaps, I was just making a fuss about Primrose and Bianca. The only problem really was the hour and a half after school before Mum or Dad got home. Could it really be as bad as all that?

OK, so maybe Primrose and Bianca said mean things to me and hogged the TV, but I wasn't scared of them. I was careful around Bianca but that was just sensible, like when a new dog comes into the kennels and you know it's got a history of biting.

You don't aggravate a biter, and Bianca actually does bite if the stories about her are true. Ellie in my class says she bit her big sister in a fight over some boy in Year 9. She saw the tooth-marks and everything.

I had settled into thinking I should put up and shut up by the time Primrose and Bianca came back from the beach. But the first thing Bianca said to me was, 'Lost any more dogs today, Pea-brain?' She laughed and Primrose joined in. How could they, when they knew how upset I had been all the time Lollie was missing?

All the mean things they had ever said to me came flooding back, and then I knew that Mum and Dad were wrong. No-one should have to put up with people being horrible to them like that, even if they can cope with it, even if it might blow over soon.

Becky was right – I had to make Mum and Dad understand just how mean Bianca and Primrose were being. But this time, I needed to choose my moment better.

I went to my bedroom to think about it. I could see Mum and Dad from my window. They had moved two garden chairs into the small patch of sunshine in the corner of the yard and were sitting there, drinking tea. They weren't busy or stressing about work today. Could the perfect time be now?

Yes, I thought, *it could*! But you know what it's like when you've decided to tell your mum and dad something really big and important. You want to work out the best way to say it first. The words fall into all different sentences inside your head like lottery balls that aren't quite making the right combinations.

In the end you wander half-heartedly out into the back yard, hoping that by the time you get there you'll know exactly how to put it, but before you can open your mouth your mum says, 'Would you like one of these?'

Mum handed me a bag of cookies. 'Bianca brought them for us from her uncle's shop,' she goes.

'She's a nice girl, isn't she?' says Dad.

The cookies were those lovely big chewy ones with white choc chips, but I shook my head. If I tried to eat one I knew I would choke on it. Mum and Dad looked at each other in surprise. 'Are you feeling all right, Peony?' they said.

No, I was not feeling all right. I couldn't try to tell again now, not while they were in full gush about how great Bianca was. The perfect moment had been snatched away. I felt like someone who had got the winning number and then lost the ticket down the drain.

'This yard could be quite nice if we got some proper plants in it,' said Dad.

'What do you mean, proper plants?' Mum bristled.

'Ones that aren't half-dead and droopy. In fact,'

goes Dad, 'how come all the plants at the Green Fingers Garden Centre keep keeling over?'

Mum frowned. It was a bit mysterious, she agreed. And even more mysterious that as soon as she brought them home they started to get better.

'Of course, the ones indoors do best,' she said. 'The front of the house is so sunny, and plants need plenty of sunlight.'

'People need sunlight too,' said Dad.

This was something he mentioned from time to time but he wasn't one to waste his energy having full-on arguments. It always made me think of that science experiment you do at school when you grow one lot of beans in a jar on a sunny window-sill and another lot in a shoe-box in the dark. The window-sill beans grow green and bushy, but the shoe-box beans grow long and spindly, and as pale as a piece of string.

In our house, Mum's plants got the window-sills and blocked the sunlight out, so we were like the beans in the shoe box. I hoped Mum knew what she was doing.

'People can move around,' laughed Mum. 'If we aren't getting enough sunlight we can always go and find some.'

'Good idea,' goes Dad. 'Let's dig out the Frisbee and hit the beach.'

They made me go too. Mum and Dad love playing games but grown-ups mostly don't play games on their own, so they always want me or Primrose to join in. That way, they can pretend they're only doing it for us.

As we walked down to the beach, the three of us, I kept thinking, 'If only it could always be just Mum and Dad and me.'

Chapter 6

The Day of the Triffids and Mr Kaminski's very green greenhouse

The mystery of the sick plants was solved the very next day. Mum came home from work fuming. She dumped her bag and stormed straight back up the zig-zag path with the wheelbarrow. As soon as she arrived back, Primrose and Bianca shot through on their way to the beach like rats leaving a sinking ship.

'Give me a hand with these spider plants, Peony,' said Mum. No 'please' or anything. Charming!

There were eight of them, so we had to make several journeys up and down the steps. We put them on the kitchen floor, just inside the door. They looked like a giant-size shaggy brown doormat that had gone nuts and sprouted.

'Aren't they supposed to be green?' I asked.

'Yes, they're supposed to be green!' snapped Mum. 'And they used to be green. Oh, they used to be green, all right! They used to be super-green because that's the way we make them at the Green Fingers Garden Centre!'

I didn't have a clue what she was talking about. I backed towards the stairs muttering about it being nearly Neighbours time. But Mum was bursting to tell someone and I was the only someone around. There was no stopping her.

'Harold was off work today so I had to do the watering. "Give them a double dose of Magic Max Plant Food with it," goes Mr Pryce. "But they only had some yesterday," I tell him.'

I tried to look as if I had a clue what she was on about.

'You're only supposed to feed plants once a week,' Mum explained impatiently. 'It seems we've been feeding all the plants every single day! We've been force-feeding them so they'll look super-healthy and sell quickly but if they don't sell they get stressed out and die of exhaustion.'

'So when you bring them home,' I ventured, 'they get better all on their own because you aren't feeding them?'

'Got it in one,' said Mum.

'Didn't you tell Mr Pryce that feeding them so much is killing them?'

'Of course I did. But he said, "I don't give a flying fig – they're plants, not pets!" And then he told me that if I didn't like it, I could leave.'

'So... are you going to leave?'

'I wish!' said Mum. 'And I would, if we didn't need the money.'

I put the kettle on. Mum loves it when I make her a cup of tea and I thought it might calm her down. I put two mugs out, then added a third because I heard Dad coming down the path. He took the steps two at a time and burst in. He had to swerve to miss the spider plants.

'Not again, Jan!' he cried. 'This can't go on. It's like the Day of the blooming Triffids in this house!'

'What does that mean?' I asked. 'What's a triffid?'

'Nothing,' goes Mum. 'Dad's being silly.'

Dad ignored her, and said to me, 'The Day of the Triffids is a book about some plants that take over the whole world.'

We both looked at Mum.

'Oh, all right!' she said. 'I'll put them outside.'

Dad pointed out that there wasn't any room outside. The yard was already chock-a-block and anyway, she'd have to get them past the half-dead cheese-plant by the back door first.

'I've had enough,' said Dad. 'I've seriously had enough! They've all got to go!'

'Go where?' Mum demanded.

'Not my problem,' goes Dad. 'And if it was, I wouldn't know the answer anyway. It seems I don't know the answer to anyone's problems. Not according to my look-at-me-suddenly-I'm-a-lifestyle-expert editor!'

Mum seized the opportunity to change the subject from plants to problems.

'So he didn't like your first Dear Daphne page, then?' she said.

'According to him, even though it's true you can't always have what you want, that isn't what people expect to hear. They expect to hear they can have what they want. When I said that was just plain stupid, he gave me a heap of Daphne's books and a list of websites and told me to do some research.'

Research sounded a bit like hard work. No wonder Dad wasn't happy. Mum tried to keep him talking while she subtly moved the spider plants towards the edge of the room with her foot. Out of sight, out of mind.

But Dad wasn't having any of it. 'Those pathetic specimens have got to go,' he said. 'I'm not backing down this time. They have to go, and so do all the rest. End of.'

I noticed a movement outside the back windows. It was Mr Kaminski shuffling up his garden path. He was wearing the same old cardigan he always wore that his wife knitted for him the winter before she died. It had a button missing and a hole in the elbow with bits of wool dangling down.

'I've got an idea!' I exclaimed. 'We could ask Mr Kaminski if he'd mind us using his greenhouse. There's nothing in it and there'd be loads of room.'

Mr Kaminski's garden rose steeply up the slope behind our house and we could see his greenhouse from our back windows. It was quite big, and literally green. The glass panes were green, with ridges of moss growing along the edges. It looked old and uncared-for, like the rest of the garden. Like Mr Kaminski himself.

Dad looked keen. Mum looked doubtful.

'I don't know,' she said. 'Mr Kaminski keeps himself to himself these days. What if he doesn't want us to use his greenhouse, but feels too embarrassed to say no?'

'I'd say that's a result,' said Dad.

He looked her straight in the eye. My dad, who was always so laid back, was fired up and determined to dig his heels in. Mum looked as surprised as I was. She seemed to think about it for a few minutes. Then she suddenly decided that, as he wasn't going to back down, she would have to. Or at least, she'd have to humour him until he'd had time to calm down.

'OK, I'll ask him next time I see him.'

'You can see him right now,' said Dad. Then, as she still didn't move, he added, 'Or I'm free right now for a trip to the dump.'

Mum frowned. She couldn't get out of it. She went out into the yard and coo-eed Mr Kaminski over the fence. We saw them talking but we couldn't hear what they were saying. After a few minutes, she came back inside.

'He said yes!' she announced.

'Fantastic!' goes Dad.

'So I said, when could we move the plants in, and he said, whenever we're ready.'

'Double fantastic!' goes Dad.

'So then I said, "That's handy because Dave's really keen and he's told me he's free right now. He'll be straight round with a brush and a bucket."'

'What, me?' goes Dad, scandalised. 'Why can't you do it? They're your plants.'

'I can't do it because I've invited Mr Kaminski round for supper. It seemed the least we could do.'

She pulled her recipe book out and started flicking through it.

'I'm sure Peony will give you a hand if you ask her nicely!'

Chapter 7
How to get what you want and Mum's famous gooseberry crumble
(these two things are not related)

Mr Kaminski's garden was like a jungle. Dad said that somewhere underneath all the overgrown bushes and weeds there had once been a pond, a birdbath, two stone angels and a patio.

'Mr and Mrs Kaminski used to sit out here all the time,' he said. 'We often got chatting over the garden wall. But when his wife died, Mr Kaminski went into his shell.'

It made me think of a sad old snail.

'Do you think he might come out of his shell again one day?' I asked.

Dad nodded. 'I reckon this might be just the nudge he needs.'

Mr Kaminski did come outside to watch for a while as we cleared all the rubbish out of the greenhouse. He said he had some planks we could use to rig up some shelves if we needed more space.

Mr Kaminski spoke with a foreign accent and his voice was very quiet. I couldn't remember ever hearing him speak before, so maybe us borrowing his greenhouse really might have given him the nudge he needed to come out of his shell, like Dad said. But knowing what our family mealtimes could be like, asking him to supper might just nudge him right back in.

On the upside, Bianca couldn't stay and eat with us because it was her brother's birthday. On the downside, Mum had decided to cook a quiche. Mum's pastry is bad enough even if you've got all your teeth, but I could see that Mr Kaminski was struggling. He had to put so much energy into chewing that he didn't have any left over for talking.

'Thank you so much for letting us use your greenhouse,' said Mum.

Mr Kaminski nodded and chewed.

'We were heading for a big row earlier,' Dad said.

'Well, we'd both had a difficult day,' said Mum.

Mr Kaminski chewed and nodded.

Dad explained about having to be Daphne and his editor telling him his first problem page was no good.

'I've got all these letters from people complaining about their lives, and I can't stand complainers!' complained Dad. 'But did I tell them they were a bunch of losers? No, I did not! I simply said they might like to stop whinging and get a life.'

'Maybe that's not so much solving problems as ignoring them?' suggested Mum.

Dad gave her a look.

'Ignore anything for long enough and it goes away,' he said.

We all joined Mr Kaminski in chewing and nodding. According to Dad's reasoning, that should've been the best way to get him to shut up. No such luck.

'There's Frustrated Fan who wants his girlfriend to like tennis and Sad Soprano who wants to be a star;

there's some woman who wants next door's cat to stop peeing in her garden and some guy who wants not to be scared of doorknobs. Well, you can't always have what you want. That's life!' said Dad.

Mr Kaminski chewed and swallowed. I noticed he wasn't nodding any more.

'Ed says I have to give these people stupid advice,' Dad went on. 'I have to tell them they can have what they want!'

'Well, of course,' said Mr Kaminski.

Dad gawped at him.

'You can have what you want!' declared Mr Kaminski. 'You just have to know how. This I learn from my mother when I am little boy in Poland.'

Mum put on her polite look. Dad was still gawping. Primrose glanced at me and raised her eyebrows.

'So, will you tell us the secret?' asked Mum. 'How can we get what we want?'

'Secret is very simple,' said Mr Kaminski. He took another mouthful of quiche. We were in for a wait. When he eventually told us, it was a bit disappointing.

'You have to be exact,' he said. 'Not wish-washy. You have to know exactly what you want.'

There was a long pause.

'Is that it?' asked Dad. You could tell he wasn't impressed, though he was trying not to show it.

'It certainly is simple,' said Mum.

'Is more,' said Mr Kaminski. 'When you know exactly what you want, you must think about it, dream about it, you must believe that you can have it.'

Another long pause.

'And that's all?' said Dad. 'That's how you get what you want?'

Mr Kaminski nodded. He suddenly turned to Mum.

'What do you want right now?' he asked.

Mum sighed. 'Right now, I want a new job,' she said. 'I don't want to go on working for that vile plant-poisoner, Mr Pryce.'

'So...' goes Mr Kaminski. 'You would rather work in office? You would like to be hairdresser?'

Mum said no – she would still want to work with plants. Except the Green Fingers Garden Centre was the only one for miles around, so that wasn't going to happen.

'Is only important to know what you want. Not to worry about how you can get it.'

'All right then,' said Mum. 'I want to stop working for Mr Plant-poisoner Pryce and get a new job, but still work with plants.'

'Now write that down,' said Mr Kaminski.

While Mum was finding a pen and paper he asked Dad, 'What do you want right now, Dave?'

'I want to stop being Daphne,' said Dad. 'But that would mean she'd have to come back and we still don't even know where she's gone.'

Mr Kaminski said Dad should write his wish down too. Then he asked me. I thought I had better not say what I wanted. 'I want to be an only child' might not go down well at a family meal.

'It's obvious what Peony wants,' said Primrose. 'She wants a dog. She's always wanted a dog. Like she's ever going to get one!'

Mum and Dad looked as if they were suddenly going off this whole idea, but Mr Kaminski ignored them and made me write it down. Then he asked Primrose what she wanted.

'She wants to be a pop star,' I said, getting my own back.

'No I don't, stupid!'

'Yes you do. I've heard you and Bianca talking about it.'

She gave me a poisonous look.

'If I want anything,' she said haughtily, 'I want to stop being called Primrose. It's a silly name. All my friends call me Annabel!'

While Mum and Dad and me picked our chins up off the table, Mr Kaminski got her to write it down. He said that if we thought about what we wanted and

59

really believed we could have it, then practical ideas about how we could go about getting it would just naturally occur to us.

'Although sometimes,' he said, 'a wish will come true without you needing to do anything. Is like magic!'

Mum asked Mr Kaminski what he wanted for himself. I thought he would probably want the rest of his quiche to disappear. Unless he had seen that it was Mum's famous gooseberry crumble for pudding. Whoever decided that gooseberries were edible? 'It's sour enough to take the top off your tongue and it's covered with bristles – hmm... let's call it a fruit!'

Mr Kaminski said he was too old to dream. He took life as it came, these days. Not much bothered him, he said. Then he ate two helpings of crumble, which kind of proved his point.

After he had gone, Mum said we shouldn't take what he had said too literally. He hadn't really meant to suggest, for example, that I might get an actual dog. He had meant something similar to having a dog might happen, something like my work at the kennels.

'Or he might have meant you could get a pet similar to a dog. A goldfish, maybe,' said Dad. 'Would you like a goldfish, Peony?'

Primrose laughed.

'I don't know what you're laughing at, Annabel!' said Dad.

Chapter 8
Mr Plant-poisoner Pryce
and the pencil-tin

When I got home from school the next day, Bianca and Primrose were out in the yard. It looked a lot bigger now it wasn't full of half-dead plants. They had changed out of their school uniform and were cooking marshmallows on wooden skewers over a disposable barbecue. They must have bunked off early and walked home via the shops in the Parade.

'None for you, Peony Podge!' said Bianca. 'You already look like jelly on legs.'

Primrose laughed. Bianca pulled the marshmallow off her skewer and popped it into her mouth. 'Mmm... gorgeous!' she said, licking her fingers. She glanced back at me. 'Are you still there? Goodbye!'

I ran up to my room. I could hear them laughing and larking about. If I went to the window, I would be able to see them, but then they might see me too. I hated them. I wished they could both vanish into thin air and never come back. Then I would have the whole yard to myself, to cook marshmallows and do anything I liked.

But when I imagined that, it felt quite lonely. Did I really want them both to disappear forever? I realised in a flash that I had not been clear about what I wanted at all – I had not been exact!

I had made a 'Free to anyone who will have her' poster about Primrose, I had wished I could be an only child and then I had wished that Primrose and Bianca could both vanish into thin air. But none of those things were exactly what I wanted. Exactly what I wanted was to get rid of Bianca and have the old Primrose back.

OK, the old Primrose wasn't perfect. Before she turned into a Pit Bull I used to think that if she was a dog she would be a Pekinese. I had a picture of one on my wall. It had a shaggy fringe tied with a pink ribbon and it seemed to be looking down its nose at everyone – which was quite an achievement as it had hardly any nose to look down.

It can be a pain living with a Pekinese. The Bumper Book of Dogs says they can be 'wilful and difficult to train'. But they're playful too. They're 'friendly and fun'. That's what Primrose used to be like, sometimes annoying and sometimes amazing, before she turned full-time snarly.

I found a piece of paper and wrote:

I want to get rid of Bianca and have the old Primrose back.

Looking at it in this way changed everything.

Now that I knew exactly what I wanted, I suddenly knew exactly what I should say to Mum and Dad. It was like Mr Kaminski had said – when you knew exactly what you wanted then you started to see what you had to do to make it happen.

I wouldn't say 'Primrose and Bianca are being horrible to me' like the first time I told – parents never listen when you tell on your sisters and brothers anyway, that's a well-known fact. I would say 'Bianca is being mean and Primrose isn't sticking up for me.'

They would believe that. They knew what Primrose was like.

The thing about Primrose is she always changes to be the same as whoever she's hanging out with. When it was Josie she was a sports fiend and all she talked about was fitness training and high-energy drinks. When it was Mushy Marcus she was into lovey-dovey DVDs and gooey looks – cringe central, but a trillion times better than how she was now, with Bianca.

I waited impatiently for Mum to come home but when she did she was in a real state. I asked her what the matter was. But she just said, 'I don't want to talk about it.'

Dad tried when he came home, and even Primrose had a go after Bianca had left, but no-one could find out what was wrong. Mum didn't say anything all the way through tea. Then she gave a great sigh and it all came out.

'That slip of paper – the one I wrote my wish down on – well, I forgot it was in my pocket. I pulled out my tissue to blow my nose and it flew out and landed at Mr Pryce's feet.'

We all looked at each other. This didn't sound good.

'He read it and then he said, "So you don't like working for Mr Plant-poisoner Pryce! Well, I think you had better leave." Just like that!'

'What did you say?' asked Dad.

'What could I say? He had given me the sack.'

'Looking on the bright side,' Primrose said, 'at least this means you won't be bringing sick plants home any more. Mr Kaminski's greenhouse is full, and it's nice not living in a jungle.'

Dad glared at her. She ignored him.

'And less plants means more room for Peony's new dog to run around in!'

All of us glared at her.

'I was only saying!' she said.

'Well, don't,' snapped Mum.

I didn't care. 'I want a dog' was just something they made me write down. I never seriously thought it could happen. My real wish was the secret one that was lying on my desk upstairs.

Dad tried to make Mum feel better.

'Everything will be all right,' he said.

'Yes? And how are we going to pay the bills, tell me that!'

He muttered something about a nice cup of tea and got up to put the kettle on. I had a feeling even tea wasn't going to work its mysterious magic this time.

'Actually,' said Dad, hovering at a safe distance by the kettle, 'when you think about it, this is the first part of your wish. You said you wanted to stop working at the Green Fingers Garden Centre – and now it's come true!'

'Oh, for goodness' sake,' said Mum. Her chair scraped across the floor as she stood up. 'I need some air.'

With that she disappeared out into the yard and we were left looking at each other like lemons. Dad shrugged. 'Would either of you girls like a cup of tea?'

I ran upstairs while he was pouring. I grabbed the piece of paper off my desk and looked around for somewhere to hide it. After what happened to Mum, I didn't want anyone to find out about my secret wish.

My pencil tin! Primrose had been known to help herself to pens or pencils in the past but she would never look in there these days because she had completely stopped doing homework. I folded the paper and put I want to get rid of Bianca and have the old Primrose back safely in the tin.

Primrose and me helped Dad to tidy up the tea things without arguing. When we had just about finished, Mum came back indoors. She had been talking to Mr Kaminski over the fence. 'The weirdest thing just happened,' she said. 'He's offered me a job!'

Mr Kaminski had decided it was time he did something about his garden. He asked Mum if she knew any good gardeners. Mum told him she didn't. She said she would have asked around at the Green Fingers Garden Centre but, as of today, she didn't work there any more.

'Is perfect!' Mr Kaminski said. 'I need gardener, you need job. And I will pay, of course!'

Mum stood there grinning. This was an unexpected turn of events and the rest of us needed a moment to take it in.

'Say something!' she said.

'That's the second part of your wish,' Dad exclaimed. 'Well, knock me down and call me Susan!'

It was what all of us were thinking, except the Susan bit. I really don't know where that came from.

Chapter 9
Ditching Daphne
and don't talk about the dog

Dad was so fired up by the surprise success of Mum's exact wish, it got him thinking about his own, and suddenly he knew what he had to do. Just because Daphne had ignored all Ed's calls to her mobile, that didn't mean she would necessarily refuse to speak to Dad.

'Nothing ventured, nothing gained' – that's another

thing Dad likes to say, so long as it's someone else doing the venturing, of course.

Anyway, instead of hitting sofa+remote as usual, Dad picked up the phone. He got Daphne's number from Ed, then dialled and waited, tapping his fingers on the edge of the table.

'I don't suppose she'll... Oh, Daphne! I-it's Dave.'

She didn't seem to know who he was because the next thing he said was, 'From work. The sports reporter.'

If she had known it was someone from the paper ringing, maybe she wouldn't have picked up. If he had known she was going to pick up, maybe he would have planned what he was going to say before he dialled.

He covered the mouthpiece with his hand and looked desperately at Mum.

'"We're worried about you,"' she hissed. '"We just want to know you're all right."'

'But...'

'Just say it!'

Dad put on his best care-y-share-y face in the hope that his voice would come out right. It didn't. I thought we were all going to drown in treacle.

'Everyone at the Three Towns Gazette is really worried about you, Daphne,' he said. Mum rolled her eyes. He ignored her and ploughed on. 'We don't even know where you are!'

The second bit came out more whiny than care-y-share-y, so he gave up trying to do it Mum's way and walked over to the window, turning his back as if to say, 'I don't need your help any more – I can take it from here!'

Daphne said something and then Dad blurted out, 'You're on the island of Capri? ... Oh, right... I see. I didn't even know you were engaged!'

There was a wail from the other end so loud we could all hear it. Dad held the phone away from his ear. When she stopped wailing, he put it back.

'You were meant to be getting married on the beach?' he said. 'Your fiancé didn't show up? Um...'

He looked as dithery as a dog that's cornered a hedgehog.

'D-did you at least get a good swim?' he asked.

Daphne let out another long wail. Dad knew he had said the wrong thing, but then his face lit up as it dawned on him what would have been the right thing to say.

'It's not the end of the world, Daphne – there are plenty more fish in the sea!'

Mum dropped her head in her hands.

'What?' said Dad, covering the mouthpiece again.

'He's already left her and I'm trying to cheer her up. You said that was all right. Make your mind up!'

He decided to cut to the chase.

'The thing is, Daphne – we miss you in the office. We need you. When are you coming back?'

Her answer sent Dad into a flat spin.

'You can't mean that!' he cried. 'Never say never, that's what you tell the readers. Ed's making me write your page. I can't do it, Daphne. What? No, I'm not just being lazy! How could she say that to me?' Dad asked us, not bothering to cover the mouthpiece. Nobody met his eye.

Dad explained to Daphne that it wasn't the extra work he was worried about – he was just really bad at giving advice. He appealed on behalf of all the good people of the Three Towns who had problems and needed her wonderful words of wisdom. He pleaded and grovelled. When that didn't work, he tried threats.

'Ed isn't going to keep your job open forever you know. If you don't hurry up and get back here you might find someone else – not me, someone proper – sitting behind the Dear Daphne desk!'

That's when she hung up on him.

'Can you believe that?' goes Dad.

Mum put her hand on his shoulder. 'You tried,' she said, soothingly.

True to his motto of 'If at first you don't succeed, give up,' Dad went straight from fired-up and hopeful to down in the dumps. He said that Mum getting what she wanted must have been a fluke and come to think of it, doing Mr Kaminski's garden wasn't really a proper job anyway, was it?

Mum got up and grabbed her gardening gloves.

'I can't sit around here all evening,' she said. 'I've got work to do.'

Dad didn't even seem to notice he'd offended her. He opened his briefcase and took out the pile of letters and emails again. They were getting a bit tatty round the edges. He shuffled through them half-heartedly.

'I haven't been this stuck since History GCSE,' he said, gloomily. 'Only that was just one exam and this could go on forever.'

'Well, until Friday, anyway,' goes Primrose, helpfully. 'I mean, that's your deadline, isn't it?

'That's this week's deadline,' goes Dad. 'What if Daphne never comes back? What if Ed refuses to get someone else in to do her work? What if I have to face this torture every single week?'

I couldn't resist. 'That's a lot of "what ifs", Dad,' I said.

Well, Friday came and he still hadn't done it. He had skimmed some of Daphne's books and was starting to talk like her, but he hadn't come up with any answers.

'This is very bad for my self-esteem,' he complained, sprawling on the sofa among his dog-eared letters and emails. Mum ignored him. She was trying to watch The Victorian Kitchen Garden, which is hard to concentrate on at the best of times. Being ignored probably wasn't very good for Dad's self-esteem either.

Primrose was hanging around, waiting for Bianca to arrive. They were having a sleep-over. The only thing keeping me going was the fact that it would soon be Saturday.

Dad read Sad Soprano's letter for the umpteenth time, just loud enough to be annoying. 'So she hasn't had the breaks,' he muttered to himself. 'Is that my fault? No! So how come I've got to sort it out for her?'

I could see he was driving Mum nuts and she was seriously about to scream at him. It was almost a relief when Bianca walked in.

'Whassup?' she said.

'Save yourself while you still can,' mumbled Mum.

But it was too late. Dad launched into the whole sorry story of how his editor had rejected his first Dear Daphne page even though he had tried his hardest and given very sensible advice, and how now he was completely stumped. She humoured him. Well, she would, what with being such a suck-up and all.

'It's obvious,' she said, reading through his first Dear Daphne. 'Sad Soprano needs to get herself on The X Factor. You're never too old these days.'

'What if she sounds like a cat in a mangle?' goes Dad.

'Not your problem,' said Bianca.

Dad seemed to consider this. He liked Bianca's approach. 'What about Frustrated Fan?' he said. 'Any ideas?'

She didn't hesitate. 'Chocs and wine,' she said. 'When his girlfriend comes round and he's got the tennis on, he wants to lay on lots of chocs and wine. Then she'll associate watching tennis with nice things. That's science.'

'Gosh!' said Dad.

They rattled through the other problems with Bianca telling Dad what to write and him jotting things down.

'This is great!' he kept saying. 'This is brilliant!'

'You know, Annabel and me could do this for you every week if you like, until the real Daphne comes back,' said Bianca. What a weasel! 'We read all the problem pages, don't we, Annabel?'

Primrose didn't look especially keen. Mum dragged herself away from The Victorian Kitchen Garden long enough to remark that Dad couldn't expect a couple of fifteen-year-olds to write a column in a respected newspaper and besides, weren't people's problems supposed to be confidential?

'I don't have to show them the actual letters,' said Dad. 'I could just ask them in theory, what would you advise this or that person to do. You've got to admit they're good. They're better than me!'

Mum didn't argue with that. She shrugged and went back to her programme. It had just hit a particularly riveting bit about how to prune fruit trees.

'This is my wish come true!' Dad suddenly exclaimed. 'I thought the only way I could get out of being Daphne was if I could persuade her to come back, but finding someone else to think of what to write – that works just as well! Thank you, Bianca, and thank you... Annabel.'

It made me sick the way he pandered to Primrose over this silly name business. Ever since she had told us she wanted to be called Annabel he hadn't called her Primrose once.

'Now we've all got what we want,' said Primrose, 'except Peony. It's a shame.' She did a much better job of pretending to care than Dad had done with Daphne.

'What did Peony want?' asked Bianca.

Mum and Dad looked uncomfortable. Primrose said, lowering her voice to a theatrical whisper, 'She wanted a dog, but that isn't going to happen so we'd better not talk about it.'

I didn't want to give them the satisfaction but I couldn't help looking gloomy. It wasn't about the dog – I had always known that was a waste of time, wish-wise. It was because the chance of my real wish coming true had just been sliced in half.

There was no way Dad would help me get rid of Bianca now he thought she was the answer to his prayers. The only chance I had left was Mum.

Chapter 10
Poor Lollie
and Becky's brainwave

Becky was waiting for me on the pavement outside her house in the morning sunshine, bouncing a tennis ball. When I got close enough, she threw it to me, and we played catch all the way to the end of the close.

As we were going through the gate into the field, she asked me how my week had been. I told her it had been weird.

She put the ball in the pocket of her shorts.

'I'm all ears!' she goes.

By the time we got to the stile on the far side of the field I had told her everything – about Ed hating Dad's first try at the problem page and Mr Kaminski telling us how to get what we want and us all writing it down. About my two wishes, the one they thought I wanted and the secret one hidden in the pencil tin.

I told her about Mum getting what she wanted almost straight away, as if by magic, and Primrose thinking she had too, though there was no way I was ever going to call her Annabel even if Mum and Dad had decided to go along with it.

I told her about Dad thinking he had got his wish, so long as it turned out Ed liked the answers Bianca had come up with.

'I see what you mean about weird,' said Becky.

We clambered over the stile and nearly bumped into Matt, who was striding down the lane.

'Hello, you two!' he goes. 'You're in for a nice surprise today.'

'What kind of surprise?'

'Well, let's just say that if you want a lolly you won't have to come all the way down to the caff to get one!'

He didn't stop, but carried straight on down the

hill, chuckling to himself. We ran the rest of the way to the kennels and as we reached the yard we heard a familiar bark.

'Lollie!' goes Becky. 'What's she still doing here?'

Lollie had her front paws up against the gate of her pen and her tail was wagging so hard she kept nearly falling over. We went inside and made a big fuss of her. Mrs Teverson must've heard the commotion because she soon came over.

She told us Lollie's owner had never turned up. She had been trying to get hold of him all week but he seemed to have left a false address.

'People do that sometimes,' she said. 'I suppose they think if they can't cope with their dogs any more it's better to leave them at a kennels than dump them in a ditch. At least that way they'll get looked after.'

Becky and I grinned at each other.

'Only it doesn't work like that,' Mrs Teverson went on. 'We kennel-owners can't take in every waif and stray that gets left behind or we'd be over-run.'

'So what's going to happen to Lollie?' asked Becky.

'We'll keep her for a few weeks and then if no-one comes to claim her we'll try to re-home her. If we can't re-home her we'll try the shelter, but if the shelter hasn't got room...' She shrugged.

We all knew what the end of that sentence would

be. 'If the shelter hasn't got room we'll have to take her to the vet's.'

'Anyway, you two can play with her as usual today after you've done the other dogs, all right?'

Mrs Teverson went back to cleaning out the segregated pens and left us alone with Lollie. She had stopped jumping around and was sitting close to the gate, looking up at us. We weren't grinning any more.

'Poor Lollie,' I said.

She sat still and let us stroke her.

'Poor Lollie,' agreed Becky.

Lollie put her head on one side as if to say, *what are you talking about*? She put her head on the other side, and then rolled right over onto her back. She didn't seem at all upset about being abandoned. 'Come on,' she seemed to say, wriggling around. 'Tickle my tummy!'

We cleaned out the pens and walked the other dogs, and when we had finished we took Lollie for a walk together. There wasn't anyone else in the three meadows so we let her off the lead and threw the tennis ball for her. She kept losing it in the long grass.

'You know,' said Becky, 'I might have an idea.'

Becky said that Lollie was an adorable dog and therefore anyone who saw her would a hundred per cent definitely fall in love with her. She was also a soft, daft, friendly and quite little dog. No-one could possibly be scared of her, not even a person who had been bitten on the bum by a dog at the age of nine.

'If we could get your dad to come up here and meet Lollie...'

I stopped her right there.

'My dad would rather jump off a cliff than set foot in a kennels.'

'Well yes, normally,' said Becky. 'But what if he thought you needed him?'

Becky's plan was simple. Next Saturday, when we knew Mum would be at work, she would phone Dad and tell him I had fallen over and hurt my ankle. It wasn't life-threatening or anything, she would say, but I was very upset and couldn't put any weight on my foot, so could he please come up right away and collect me?

'Then you can go and hide in the barn, and I'll wait for your dad out the front with Lollie. When your dad arrives, I'll say you're just finding a bandage or something, and get him talking about Lollie while we're waiting. I'll tell him what a lovely and completely non-dangerous dog she is, and about her being abandoned, and what's going to happen to her if no-one offers to take her in.'

I must have not looked very convinced because then Becky said, 'Oh, come on, Peony. He'd have to have a heart of stone to resist such a sweet dog with such a sad story!'

Lollie came bounding back with the ball. I threw it again for her. She went haring after it, ran too far and then bounced around in the long grass, trying to find it.

'He hasn't got a heart of stone,' I said. 'But he has got legs of jelly whenever he's anywhere near a dog.'

Becky ignored my objection and went on with her plan.

'I'll say, "Hold onto this while I go and find Peony for you." Then I'll put the lead in his hand and leave them to it.'

'He'll freak,' I said. 'Seriously.'

'Yeah, but surely it's worth a try?' goes Becky.

Lollie gave up looking for the ball and came back without it, so Becky and me had to go searching for it ourselves.

'When you think about it,' Becky said, 'everyone else in your family seems to be getting what they want, so why shouldn't it work for you?'

I pointed out that I never had really believed I could have a dog – it was the other wish I had been focusing on.

'Well, maybe that's already sorting itself out but you haven't realised it yet,' said Becky. 'I mean, with your mum working just the other side of the garden fence, Primrose and Bianca won't have to hang around after school so-called looking after you, will they? Plus if they do hang around, they won't be able to blast your eardrums with bad singing and all that.'

She was right, I hadn't thought about this. I wasn't exactly getting rid of Bianca but I was almost certainly going to be seeing a lot less of her. There was no denying that was a step in the right direction.

Becky found the ball.

'If one wish works,' she said, 'why not two?'

So when I got home I found the piece of paper I had written I **want a dog** on and just to be exact I added, **Actually, I want Lollie.** Then I folded it a few times and put it in my pencil tin along with **I want to get rid of Bianca and have the old Primrose back.**

Chapter 11
Two-faced tricksters and sugar sandwiches

The day Mum started work on Mr Kaminski's garden felt like the first day of the rest of my life. It wasn't perfect, but it was much better. I seriously thought a bit of Mum's wish-magic must have spread in my direction.

Mum popped over the fence to say hello when she heard us arriving home from school, and that meant Primrose and Bianca couldn't say mean things to me or push me around. Bianca still pulled faces when Mum's back was turned, and she puffed out her cheeks and mouthed the word 'hippo' when I took a biscuit, but when Mum was looking they acted as if the three of us were all the best of friends.

I only had to put up with ten minutes of two-faced weaseliness before Primrose and Bianca went off to the beach. Mum disappeared back over the fence and I went upstairs to watch TV. Like I said, it wasn't perfect, but it was much better.

The second day was the same. Mum came over for a chat as soon as we got home. When she was looking, Bianca and Primrose were as sweet to me as the goo on a syrup pudding but as soon as her back was turned they were horrible. Then the two of them went to the beach, Mum climbed back over the fence and I had the place to myself.

The third day started the same – Mum, two-faced tricksters, empty house – but I'd only had the place to myself for about half an hour when Bianca and Primrose came back. It was too windy at the beach, they said. They fancied an afternoon at home. They plumped down on the settee on either side of me. I tightened my grip on the remote. They weren't going to switch channels in the middle of my programme, not if I could help it.

'Go away,' I said.

'That's not very friendly,' said Bianca.

'Seriously, go away.'

'But we like the Dog Whisperer. We want to watch it too.'

I glared at her.

'It's a free country,' she said.

I would have got up and left the room only I really wanted to see what was going to happen to the boxer with behavioural problems – if they couldn't get him to stop going for other dogs, he would have to be put down.

I should have left because I couldn't watch anyway, they kept talking so much. They said stupid mean things like 'That dog should be put down anyway for being so ugly,' and 'We've got enough fat slobbery creatures in the world already, nudge-nudge, wink-wink, you know who.'

I tried not to say anything. I remembered what Dad said, that if you ignore something for long enough it goes away. But I could feel my skin prickling and my body tensing up. Bianca stared at me.

'You're going red,' she said. 'I thought Peonies were

supposed to be blue.'

She pulled her phone out of her pocket. 'This is an interesting natural phenomenon. We should record it for posterity!'

She started to video me. She shoved her phone right up to my face. I tried to push it away.

'Leave me alone!' I cried.

'It speaks!' said Bianca. She turned the phone towards her own face and said in a David Attenborough whisper, 'The unusual red Peony can talk, although you will notice it has a very high, whiny voice.'

She turned it back on me. 'Say something else,' she said.

'Go away!' I yelled. I tried to grab the phone off her.

'Oooh – this is good!' cried Bianca. 'We can put it on YouTube!'

Primrose picked up the remote and started flicking the channels but Bianca went on pushing her phone in my face. I made a lunge for it. She snatched it out of the way and I fell flat on the floor. She laughed and kept filming, and then it was like this red mist came over me and I went for her.

She was bigger than me but I was madder, and I grabbed her wrist and prised her fingers open and finally I got the phone off her. She backed away suddenly, holding her arm as if I had really hurt her.

But she wasn't looking at her arm and she wasn't looking at me... she was looking towards the door.

'Peony! What on earth do you think you're doing? Give Bianca back her phone this minute!'

I stood there blinking like a rabbit in the headlights while Mum marched across the room, took the phone off me and gave it back to Bianca.

'I'm so sorry,' she said. 'I can't think what's got into Peony. Are you all right, Bianca?'

Mum turned back to me. 'I could hear you yelling from Mr Kaminski's garden. Honestly, Peony, can't I leave you for five minutes...?'

It was so unfair! I stormed upstairs to my bedroom and slammed the door. My heart was pounding. I wanted to scream, I wanted to hit something. I made my hand into a tight fist and bit the side of my finger really hard. It hurt like mad, but the pain made me calm down.

When I had stopped shaking I flopped down on the bed and lay there staring at the wall. Forty breeds of dog stared back at me. I scanned along the rows, saying their names in my head.

'One, Bassett Hound. Two, German Shepherd. Three, Cairn Terrier...'

It was what I always did when Primrose and Bianca wound me up. I read about it in this book. You can do it with anything; it doesn't have to be dogs. The book said it would work with whatever you happen to have on your wall, such as pop stars or surfers or strikers.

I got to the end and started again, and by the time I had gone round twice the dogs had pushed Primrose and Bianca towards the back of my mind. I was in the dog zone, which is the best place in the world to be.

There was a soft rat-a-tat on the door. It was Mum.

'OK to come in?'

I thought she had come to tell me off again but she had brought me a sandwich and a glass of milk which she put down on my desk. Had she realised that she'd got it wrong? Had she guessed what made me grab Bianca's phone? Was she going to help me now?

'I've put a sprinkling of brown sugar in your sandwich,' she said. 'I'm sure you'll feel better when you've had a bite to eat.'

I suddenly remembered when Primrose was in Year 6, Mum started feeding her sugar sandwiches whenever she got in a temper. She was a firm believer in sugar sandwiches as Nature's remedy for what she called 'the pre-teen ups and downs.'

Mum sat carefully on the end of my bed as if she was afraid it might suddenly open and swallow her up. When it didn't, she made herself comfortable.

'That really wasn't like you, Peony,' she said,

'brawling with Bianca and grabbing her phone. But don't worry; nobody's cross.'

Actually, somebody is cross, I thought, feeling my hackles rising again.

'It's just your age,' said Mum. 'It's an up and down time. One minute, you can be happy as honeysuckle on a hot wall and the next minute you're as sad as a soggy cactus.'

So that was that. It was no good knowing exactly the right words to say – 'Bianca is being horrible and Primrose isn't sticking up for me' – if nobody was prepared to listen. There was no point trying to tell Dad because he needed Bianca for his Daphne letters, and now there was no point telling Mum either because she was convinced that the whole problem was me.

Chapter 12
The East Lane Emporium and desperate measures

With Mum and Dad out of the picture, I lay on my bed and tried to think of another plan. That's what Mr Kaminski said you had to do. It had to be an exact plan to get rid of Bianca and have the old Primrose back.

I remembered what Bianca said about Frustrated Fan, that he should give his girlfriend chocs and wine when the tennis was on so she would associate watching tennis with lovely things. Well, why shouldn't that work the other way round? If I could make horrible things happen to Bianca every time she came to our house then surely that would put her off coming.

The obvious way to put someone off coming to your house would be to get into arguments with them, but Bianca actually liked it when I got annoyed; she thought it was funny. So I had to be more cunning and think of horrible things that seemed to have nothing at all to do with me.

I knew just where I could get some horrible things. Matt Teverson's youngest brother Justin spent all his pocket money in the East Lane Emporium on plastic dog poos and stick-on bogeys and he said they had much worse things in there that his mum wouldn't let him buy, such as skunk spray you could squirt on someone and it didn't wash off for a week.

I didn't know if Justin had made that up about the skunk spray – you could never tell with the Teversons – but it seemed like a good idea to check out the East Lane Emporium, so the next day I took a detour down there after school. I was allowed to do that now, so long as I let Mum know, which was better than when Primrose was supposed to be looking after me and we had to go straight home after school.

East Lane isn't really a shopping street and the Emporium looks like an ordinary house squashed in between lots of other ordinary houses. I nearly didn't go in, but then I remembered how much I hated Bianca and that got me right up the front steps and in through the door.

The whole shop was like some mad person's front room, crammed with jokes and tricks, costumes and masks. The man behind the counter had a bald head and a strip of beard like a thin dribble down his chin. He had tattoos all the way up his arms and a nail stuck through one ear lobe. I was really glad he ignored me and went on reading his magazine.

Most of the practical jokes were the kind of stuff that Justin loved, rubber slugs to put in someone's salad or bandages covered in fake blood. But some of them weren't really funny; they were more like mean tricks such as chewing gum that made your teeth go green.

I bought a packet of super-strong fart sweets and some itching powder. Those should make life uncomfortable for Bianca all right, and no-one need ever know what had caused her tummy upset or infuriating itch, let alone that I had anything to do with it.

There were lots more things to try as well, and everything in the East Lane Emporium was cheap – so with the money I earned working at the kennels I could keep this up for as long as it took. A brand new bad experience for Bianca at our house every day until she got the message and stopped coming.

It was a genius plan. It simply could not fail. I wasn't proud of myself for thinking of it; I would never normally do anything to hurt anyone. But desperate times call for desperate measures.

When I got home Primrose and Bianca were watching TV and Mum was hacking her way through the brambles at the top of Mr Kaminski's garden. I tipped the super-strong fart sweets into a bowl and put it in the middle of the kitchen table. I knew Primrose wouldn't take any because she had broken her brace on a hard sweet a few months before and hadn't touched one since.

I waited, and sure enough after a while they came downstairs to have a rummage in the fridge. I made sure I was on the other side of the room, nowhere near the fart sweets, so I could act surprised at seeing them on the table.

'Ooh, sweets!' I said. 'They look nice!' I took one

and pushed the bowl a few inches towards Bianca.

'I don't eat sweets,' she said, pushing it back. 'And quite honestly, Peony Pudgyface, neither should you.'

Primrose took two cold bottles of Diet Pepsi out of the fridge and shut the door. Then they grabbed their bikinis out of their beach bags, which were still lying on the floor where they had left them from last time, and went back upstairs to get changed.

It wasn't a good start, but I still had the itching powder and I had to act fast. I took Bianca's beach towel out of her bag and sprinkled the itching powder all over it. Then I carefully rolled it up again and put it back.

I had only just finished when Mum came in. She pulled off her gardening gloves, pushed her hair off her face and went straight to the kettle.

'I'm gasping for a cuppa,' she said. Then she noticed the sweets.

'Where did those come from? Proper old-fashioned boiled sweets – you know who would like them? Mr Kaminski!'

I tried to stop her. 'Do you think his teeth are up to it?' I said. 'What if he chokes on one and dies? Old people are always doing that.' But she shovelled them into her pocket, finished making her tea and disappeared back over the fence.

This was not good. This was not good at all. If Mr Kaminski liked boiled sweets he might eat them all. Just one fart sweet was supposed to make you trump like a train – if a person ate the whole packet, well, he might explode! But before I had a chance to work out how I could get them back Bianca and Primrose came bounding down the stairs.

'I've got an idea,' Primrose said as she rifled through her bag looking for her sunglasses. 'Why don't we swap towels today? Mine would go really well with your bikini and yours would go really well with mine.'

Oh, great. Oh, that's just great, I thought to myself as I watched them disappear down the zig-zag path. But I couldn't stand there feeling bad for long because I had to try and stop Mr Kaminski from eating the fart sweets. Primrose was going to get itchy, but things were looking even worse for Mr K and it was my fault.

I went out into the yard. Mum was still hacking away at the brambles and Mr Kaminski was sitting on his new deckchair on the patio she'd found under all the weeds a few days before. On the paving stone beside his foot, a small pile of empty sweet wrappers glistened in the sun.

The fart sweets couldn't have kicked in yet because Mr Kaminski looked very peaceful and not at all like someone who was about to blow up. I ran back indoors and made a big jug of iced water. If I could get him to drink lots and lots of it maybe it would flush the fart sweets out of his system before they had a chance to work.

Mr Kaminski was delighted with me for taking a drink out to him. He took a few sips and nodded in appreciation. He sipped again. I hovered with the jug but he didn't drink any faster. Sip, sip... Sip, sip...

Time ticked away and the fart sweets were not getting flushed, so in the end I gave up and went back indoors. If I couldn't prevent the worst from happening, then I certainly didn't want to be there when it did.

Mr Kaminski wasn't getting flushed... but it turned out that Primrose was. After an hour or two lying on a towel covered in itching powder she came home looking like a beetroot. Dad asked her if it was sore and Mum told her off for not using enough sun cream.

'Does it itch?' I asked.

'Sunburn doesn't itch,' Mum said, and Primrose didn't contradict her. Weird.

Now I didn't only have the fact that Mr Kaminski might blow up at any moment to worry about but also Primrose's bright red skin. What if stayed red? What if it started to go other colours or... what if it all peeled off?

I spent the rest of the evening running backwards and forwards between spying on Mr Kaminski and trying to get a close look at Primrose's skin without making her suspicious. It was worse than getting blasted by power ballads or called nasty names.

On the up side, by bed-time Mr Kaminski still didn't seem to be suffering any ill effects and Primrose's skin had faded almost back to normal. On the down side, I was a nervous wreck.

There was no doubt about it, going to the East Lane Emporium had not been a genius idea after all. It had been a stupid one. It had been more than stupid, it had been dangerous, because innocent people could have got hurt, at least if the tricks hadn't been so rubbish and had done what they were supposed to do.

I decided to check on Primrose's skin one last time before I went to bed. It was easy because she was fast asleep in front of the telly. Unlike Dad, she didn't usually snooze on the settee, and I hoped this wasn't a side effect of too much non-itching itching powder. Her phone was lying on the cushions.

Seeing it gave me the glimmer of an idea. I could send Bianca a text from Primrose's phone, saying something like 'You can't come round to my house any more.'

I picked it up and the screen saver flicked on. It was

a fuzzy picture of a boy outside the beach cafe. I knew that boy — it was Matt! What was a picture of Matt doing on Primrose's phone?

She stirred in her sleep and I put the phone back on the cushions quick-smart. Texting Bianca from Primrose's phone might be a good idea but on the other hand it might be a terrible one and I wasn't about to rush into anything, not after the day I had just had.

Chapter 13
Feeling stupid
and falling apart

The next day, Dad was home early. We found him
and Mum drinking home-made lemonade in the back
yard when we walked in. Behind them, Mr Kaminski's
garden was starting to look really nice. Our little yard
looked quite sorry for itself in comparison. There was
nothing in it except dark rings on the paving stones
where the pots and plants had been.

Dad was looking sorry for himself too. It turned out Ed wasn't happy with his second try at answering the Dear Daphne letters and he only had the weekend to come up with something better. Daphne had left a few articles on file about topics such as 'Weight Worries' and 'Losing a Loved One' that they could use instead if they had to, but you couldn't have a problem page which never actually got around to answering people's letters.

'Why wasn't he happy with it?' asked Bianca.

Dad shrugged.

'He says telling Sad Soprano to go on The X Factor might be setting her up for global humiliation if it turns out she can't sing, and if Frustrated Fan goes down the chocs-and-wine road his girlfriend will end up looking like the back of a bus. It's all nit-picking stuff like that.'

'Cat-poo lady?' asked Primrose.

'Apparently it's not OK to throw the poos over the fence, even though technically they do belong to the neighbour's cat so she'd only be returning his property.'

'Man who's scared of door-knobs?'

'Well, it seems that covering them up with paper bags is a silly idea.'

'Maybe Ed thinks some people might not find door

handles wrapped up in paper bags a very attractive design feature,' suggested Mum.

Dad ignored her. He rattled through the rest of the problem page with Bianca and Primrose. They all seemed amazed that Ed hadn't liked any of the solutions Bianca had come up with. I was secretly loving it, Dad's Official Life-Saver Bianca turning out to be completely useless.

'I told you you couldn't expect a couple of fifteen-year-olds – no offence, you two – to write a problem page in a respected newspaper, didn't I?' Mum reminded him.

'Oh, yes,' goes Dad, 'very helpful. There's nothing like "I told you so" to make a bad situation better.'

'No need to be sarcastic,' said Mum.

Primrose and Bianca sidled off.

'It's no good, Jan,' said Dad. 'I just can't do it. I'm going to have to start looking for another job in case Ed really does sack me from the sports desk over this.'

'But the Three Towns Gazette is the only newspaper around – where are you going to get another sports-reporting job?'

Dad shrugged again. He drained his glass.

'Maybe the new Daphne will be able to give me some advice,' he said bitterly.

Mr Kaminski chose that moment to come over and

show Mum a fountain he was thinking of buying from his gardening catalogue. He straight away spotted that Dad was out of sorts. Mum told him about the latest Dear Daphne development.

'But is good!' declared Mr Kaminski. 'You think of plan, you try plan, now you think again, yes?'

Mum, who was obviously Mr Kaminski's biggest fan by now, agreed.

'That's right! When you first wrote down what you wanted you thought the only way to get it was if you could make Daphne come back. That didn't work so you came up with another plan – finding someone else to do it. Which would have been fine except you chose the wrong someone.'

'I know, I know,' Dad interrupted. 'A couple of fifteen-year-olds – bad choice.'

'So when you think about it, you just need to find the right person, someone who's got a bit more of a clue about life, someone older and wiser.'

'I asked you, but you said no.'

'Well, we'd only argue about it, wouldn't we?' said Mum.

Mr K sat silently nodding his head like a scrawny old owl in a tree.

'Keep thinking about what you want, Dave. Exactly what you want. Plan will come.'

It was so true. When you thought and thought about the thing you really wanted, the plans came thick and fast. I wished I could tell them about my new idea for banishing Bianca, because the more I thought about it, the more I liked it.

I realised that sending a text from Primrose's phone which said 'You can't come to my house any more' wouldn't do – Bianca would just ask Primrose why not and Primrose would say she never sent it and then they would straight away know it was me.

But people were always falling out over texts, so it could definitely work if I could just come up with the right message. It had to be something that would make Bianca so cross she wouldn't even speak to Primrose, because then Primrose wouldn't have a chance to explain it away.

And it wasn't only my secret wish that was moving closer to coming true – there was the wish they knew about, me getting a dog. Who would have thought a few short weeks ago that I had a frog's chance in a piranha pond of getting a dog, yet the very next morning Becky's plan was about to make that happen.

I don't know how I managed to not say anything, especially with Dad being so down in the dumps, but the success of Becky's plan depended upon the element of surprise. I passed an hour or so in my bedroom practising my limp, chatted to Becky on Facebook and went to bed early so the morning would come quicker.

I was up and out of the house early, but Becky was already waiting for me in the close. She was so excited you would think it was her and not me who was getting Lollie. The sun was shining, the birds were singing in the hedges – the whole world was a hap-hap-happy place.

Mrs Teverson was surprised to see us. She checked her watch and gave it a little tap in case it had dozed off or something. 'You're early!' she remarked.

'We thought we'd play with Lollie before we start,' said Becky.

Mrs Teverson said we couldn't play with Lollie because Lollie had gone home. Her owner had come for her. He admitted that he'd intended to abandon her but in the end he couldn't do it.

'Isn't that wonderful news?' said Mrs Teverson.

Becky and I tried to smile.

'Could you start by cleaning out Lollie's pen? We've got a rough collie coming in later today.'

We got our mops and buckets from the caravan. The gate to Lollie's pen was lying open and her cupcake was caught underneath it. Her owner hadn't even bothered to make sure she had her favourite toy.

We stood in the empty pen, not saying anything. Becky touched my shoulder. Then she put her arm round me. Then she gave me a hug. I'm not normally a huggy person and maybe that's why the minute my face touched her shoulder, I burst into tears.

I'm not the kind of person who cries a lot either, except when I'm watching Homeward Bound. I don't like people who cry all the time. Sasha in our class cries every single day and I wish she would stop and give herself a chance to dry out.

But it was really weird because as we mopped out Lollie's pen and hosed it down, tears kept spilling out of me as if I had sprung a leak. I had really believed our plan would work and I would end up taking Lollie home. How could I have been so stupid?

Feeling stupid, stupid, stupid, I cleaned the pens and walked the dogs and my eyes kept suddenly leaking. I was grateful to Becky for pretending not to notice because if she were to give me another hug I was sure I would full-on fall to pieces.

She walked, I mopped; I walked, she mopped. We worked our way along the pens. When we had finished, Becky said, 'We should do something new now to cheer ourselves up. Shall we go down to the beach and get a pasty?'

That would certainly be new. We had never been

anywhere together except the kennels, what with her being older than me and everything, and I wasn't sure I really wanted to go. But Becky said she was sad too about Lollie leaving and lunch at the beach might cheer her up.

'OK,' I said. 'That would be nice. I'll phone Dad and let him know I won't be home.'

So I did, and then we walked down the hill together, me and Becky, in the baking hot sun.

Chapter 14
Cornish honeycomb ice-cream and a red rag to a bull

The tide was out and the boats in the harbour were stuck in the mud among a criss-cross of gulls' footprints and bits of rubbish. We passed a long queue of tourists outside the chip shop and carried on walking till we got to the beach. All the tables outside the Crocodile Cafe were full.

'We can get takeaway,' said Becky.

Matt was serving behind the counter but he was too

busy to talk, so we took our pasties and sat at the top of the beach. I noticed Bianca and Primrose hanging around with some other girls near the lifeguards' hut but they were too busy trying to impress the lifeguards to notice me.

We had finished our pasties and were lying down on the warm sand when Matt came over. He had two ice-cream cornets in one hand and one in the other. They were beginning to drip.

'I'm on my break and I thought my best girls might like some dessert,' he said.

We sat up, blinking in the bright sunshine.

'I've got choc chip...' said Matt, nodding towards a chocolate ice-cream with a cold chip stuck in the top. 'Or butterscotch and vanilla...' which was vanilla ice-cream with a butterscotch boiled sweet sliding slowly down it. 'Or my personal favourite, Cornish honeycomb!' You guessed – that one had a new comb from the box on the counter sticking up out of it.

We actually laughed.

'That's better,' goes Matt. 'You looked like a wet Wednesday when you first came down and that can't be right – it's a sunny Saturday! What's going on?'

We told him we were sad about Lollie leaving but we didn't tell him about Becky's plan. Well, it sounded silly now. I had the Cornish honeycomb ice-cream because I wanted to keep the comb to remind me that nice people can make you smile even when you're having a leaky day.

Out of the corner of my eye I noticed that Bianca had seen me and was pointing me out to Primrose. She said something and they both laughed. I tried to ignore them and Bianca soon lost interest, but every time I glanced across after that I caught sight of Primrose staring back at me.

What was her problem? Did she think I was following them or something? I wanted to shout out, 'I've got as much right to be on this beach as you have!'

Soon Matt's break was over and Becky had to go for her riding lesson. I walked home up the zig-zag path on my own. Dad was sitting on the front steps listening to the cricket on his MP3. He took one earphone out.

'Nice lunch?'

I nodded.

'Mum's shopping,' he said. 'She and Mr K have gone with Stella in her van to look for some garden furniture.'

Stella was Mum's friend from the Green Fingers Garden Centre. She still worked there because she needed the money, but she was looking for another job. She thought Mr Pryce was out of order giving

Mum the sack just because she called him a plant-poisoner.

When you're having an up-and-down day there's nothing like TV to even things out so I went indoors, flopped on the settee and started flicking the channels. I had just decided to go with two and a half hours of Neighbours omnibus when I heard voices outside talking to Dad.

What were Primrose and Bianca doing back from the beach so soon? I turned the volume down.

'I don't understand it,' Bianca was saying, as they dumped their stuff in the kitchen. 'I had exactly the same as you for lunch and I feel fine.'

'Thanks for walking back with me but you don't have to stay,' said Primrose, coming up the stairs. 'I think I'll just go and lie down for a bit.'

'Of course I'll stay,' goes Bianca. 'You'll probably feel better soon and we can go back down to the beach.'

They came into the room.

'Oh!' said Primrose, seeing me sprawled on the sofa.

She was bending over slightly, holding her stomach and occasionally remembering to wince as if she was in pain. I could tell she was putting it on and the way Bianca was acting, so could she.

'Where's your paracetamol?' she said impatiently. 'Two of those and you'll be right as rain, yeah?'

'I don't need paracetamol. I just need to sit down. I'm afraid I'm not going to be very good company.'

'Nothing new there then!' laughed Bianca. 'But seriously, babe, you've got to get better before tonight. It's the first time they've invited us.'

'Hmm,' I thought. 'Could that be why Primrose is faking a stomach ache? Is it just that she wants to get out of going to one of the lifeguards' famous beach parties?' It didn't seem likely.

Primrose dropped into the armchair, clutching her stomach.

'I'm so sorry but seriously, there's no way I'm going to be able to go to the party. You go though. Don't worry about me.'

'What, on my own?' cried Bianca. 'I don't think so! You can't bail on me now.'

But Primrose kept it up for two whole hours and finally Bianca had to give up and go home.

'I'll ring you tomorrow,' she said. 'Assuming you haven't died in the night, of course,' she added sarcastically. Ouch!

The minute she had gone Primrose said, 'You aren't watching this are you?' and before I had time to answer she grabbed the remote and turned the TV off.

'How do you know that boy?' she demanded.

'What boy?'

'Don't act dim. The one at the beach.'

'None of your business,' I said. 'And anyway, I thought you were supposed to be ill.'

'Whatever,' snapped Primrose.

I took the remote back and switched the TV on again. It was the adverts. Primrose still wasn't giving up.

'He's called Mac, isn't he?'

'No, actually. He's called Matt.'

'So... where did you meet him?'

'None of your business, like I said.' I turned the volume up. 'Now if you don't mind, I'm watching TV and I don't want to talk, which shouldn't be a problem because a pea-brain like me obviously can't have anything interesting to say.'

'It was just Bianca who said that. You know what she's like. She was having a laugh.'

'So were you,' I said. 'But guess what? I wasn't.'

Primrose got that frown she gets when things aren't going her way.

'I don't know what's going on with you and Bianca but don't take it out on me,' I said.

It was like a red rag to a bull.

'Right!' Primrose lunged forward and grabbed the

remote out of my hand. 'Stop messing around and tell me how you know him!'

'Why should I?'

She dangled the remote above my head, just out of reach.

'Oh, all right,' I said. 'From the kennels. He's one of the Teversons.'

I leapt up and grabbed the remote back. She laughed.

'See? That wasn't so hard, was it?'

Primrose went to her room and I tried to watch Neighbours but I couldn't concentrate. The prickly feeling behind my eyes had come back. Even if I could get rid of Bianca, what was there to say the old Primrose would come back?

So much of Bianca seemed to have rubbed off on Primrose that it felt as if she had deliberately got Bianca out the way just so she could have a go at pushing me around on her own.

Chapter 15
Way to go, Dad,
and thank you, Annabel!

The next day, Primrose told Bianca she still wasn't feeling well. On the upside, that meant Bianca didn't come round, but on the downside Primrose had nothing to do. She hates being on her own and Mum and Dad had both gone out.

'Do you want a milkshake?' she asked. 'I'm making one.'

Like I would drink anything she made for me. I didn't

even look up from my book. She went downstairs, rattled around in the kitchen and came back up again. Then she went upstairs and rattled around in her bedroom. Five minutes later, she was back.

'You can have this.' She tossed her grey hoodie onto the settee. 'It's too small for me and I know you like it.'

Was it full of itching powder or something? I pushed it away.

'What are you reading? Is it any good?'

She was like a big noisy bluebottle buzzing around, driving me mad. I put my book down.

'Why are you being weird?' I said.

'I'm not.'

'Yes you are.'

She backed off, but though she didn't try to talk to me any more she still hung around. I was glad when Mum got back from Stella's and made her go and tidy her bedroom.

Dad was at the county cricket ground watching Cornwall play Wiltshire all afternoon and he came home in such a good mood we thought Cornwall must have won by at least a trillion runs.

'So – good game?' asked Mum.

'No, they thrashed us,' said Dad, cheerfully. 'But there are more important things in life than cricket!'

He grabbed his laptop and went upstairs to write his report.

'I must be imagining things,' said Mum. 'I could swear I just heard Dad say there were more important things in life than cricket.'

It turned out that the more important thing on Dad's mind was the problem page, because if he couldn't get that right he would be out of a job and then he wouldn't get any more free tickets to the cricket – or the football or the rugby or any other sport, come to that.

It was so much on his mind that he couldn't follow the game... and then all of a sudden he had it, the answer to his prayers. Mr Kaminski! He was a person with lots and lots and lots of life experience.

Dad called in on him after the match and asked him straight out, what did he think Frustrated Fan should do?

'Is always same thing,' said Mr Kaminski. 'You have to ask, what does he want? What exactly does he want? Does he want his girlfriend to watch tennis with him? No! She will talk all the time. She will ask the rules.'

Dad nodded. He completely got that. He hated it when Mum tried to watch football with him.

'This Frustrated Fan, he wants her to let him watch

in peace. So he must do a deal. He watches tennis but on next day he takes her out, somewhere lovely, something she wants to do.'

'But he wants to watch all of Wimbledon – and that's a whole fortnight.'

'Then he take her on holiday one whole fortnight, yes?'

Mr Kaminski went through all the problems with Dad and then Dad emailed his answers straight off to Ed.

'Ed just rang and he's really happy with it – and you know the best thing?' goes Dad. 'Mr K said he wouldn't mind helping me every week until Daphne comes back, however long that will be.'

Way to go, Dad!

'You should buy him a thank-you present,' said Mum.

'I know what he needs,' piped up Primrose. 'A new cardigan!'

'That's a brilliant idea, Annabel,' goes Dad.

She put on her queen-of-smug face.

'Actually, I've had another brilliant idea as well. Peony really wants a dog, and the main reason she can't have one is because you're scared of them, right?'

Dad looked as if he might argue the point but then

decided not to because, let's face it, we all knew it was true.

'Well, you could go to the kennels and meet some dogs, and learn not to be scared any more.'

What was she playing at? Why should she want to help me get a dog? Who was this new Primrose and where had the old one gone?

Mum said, 'That *is* a good idea, Prim... I mean, Annabel.'

'Thanks. I thought, as you know Mrs Teverson, you could set it up. You could ask if she's got any little tiny dogs in at the moment that Dad could start with.'

Dad said he didn't like little tiny dogs. They yapped and jumped about and sank their teeth into people's ankles.

'OK then, big docile dogs,' said Primrose.

But Dad didn't like big docile dogs either. A big docile dog could unexpectedly get competitive over the ball and bite a person on the bum. He shuddered.

'Then how about really, really old dogs, the sort that haven't got many teeth left and can't jump up any more?'

He seemed to consider it. I couldn't see why Primrose should be trying to help me but she did seem to be on to something.

'One of the Teversons' own dogs is really,

really old,' I said. 'He's called Sam and he's nearly blind.'

'Ideal!' goes Primrose. 'Come on Dad. I'll go with you for moral support.'

'You could go on Saturday when Peony's there,' suggested Mum.

'No! Not Saturday!' Primrose said, a bit too quickly.

Suddenly, it all started to make sense.

'I-it must be very busy on Saturdays, isn't that right, Peony?'

Yes, that was right – and also, Matt wouldn't be there because he would be working at the Crocodile Cafe.

She fancied him! That was why she had a picture of him on her phone. That was why she gave Bianca the brush-off, so she could get me on my own and make me tell her everything I knew about him.

If Primrose wanted Bianca out of the way when she gave me a grilling it must be because Bianca didn't know she fancied Matt. Bianca must think Primrose was like her, hanging around at the beach because of the lifeguards, when all the time she was just after a glimpse of Matt in the cafe.

That's when I had my light-bulb moment. I saw how I could get rid of Bianca for certain sure and have the old Primrose back. If Primrose started going out with

Matt she wouldn't want to have Bianca around all the time. It would be Matt and not Bianca hanging round our house, and that would be better than better – it would be perfect!

'You're right, Primrose,' I said. 'A week-day evening would be best.'

Mum said I really should try harder to remember to call Primrose Annabel considering all the trouble she was going to, helping me to get what I wanted.

'Yes,' I said, turning to Primrose. 'It really is very generous of you doing all this, especially when there's nothing at all in it for you.'

She went bright red. Then I knew one hundred per cent that I was right.

'Thank you, Annabel!' I said.

Chapter 16
A cowardy custard and a cunning plan

Dad bottled it. Like I'd told Becky, he'd rather jump off a cliff than set foot in a kennels, even with Primrose there to hold his hand. He's such a cowardy custard.

Primrose didn't seem to have any other great ideas about how to make Matt notice her except gazing at him adoringly from a distance on the beach.

'Sometimes love needs a helping hand,' Becky said. We were having our lunch under a sun umbrella outside the Crocodile Cafe, which we had decided to do every Saturday.

Matt came out to wipe the tables. Becky said, 'See that girl down by the lifeguards' station?'

'Which one?'

'The one in the blue bikini. She fancies you.'

Matt laughed. 'Yeah, that'll be why she's always hanging around the lifeguards then.'

So he had noticed her, always hanging around.

'Really, she does,' said Becky. 'We know because she's Peony's sister.'

That got his attention.

'She's got a photo of you in her phone,' I said.

'Why don't you ask her out?' goes Becky. 'She'd definitely say yes.'

Matt did seem quite keen but you could kind of tell he wasn't going to actually ask her.

'He might be a bit too shy,' I said, after he had gone back in.

'Hmm, you could be right,' said Becky. 'Sometimes love needs an almighty shove. How can we get those two in the same room together?'

'I know,' I said. Mr Kaminski's garden-warming party!'

Mr Kaminski was having a barbecue that evening to celebrate his wonderful new garden. He had invited everyone in Harbour Row and asked us to tell our friends. I was bringing Becky.

Next time Matt came out to clear the tables we called him over and asked him. Everyone in Harbour Row would be there, we said. Including Primrose.

'I don't know,' said Matt. 'I'm helping my dad to build some new fences when I've finished here. It'll be quite late by the time that's done.'

We tried to persuade him but that just seemed to make him more sure he wouldn't be able to come.

Anyway, there was another problem. Bianca had already invited herself to the barbecue, and Matt and Primrose would never get a minute to themselves with her around. She would be sticking to Primrose like glue because the lifeguards were having another beach party later that night and this time she was determined she and Primrose were going to be there. She was still narked with Primrose for making them miss the last one.

'So...' Becky said, when I explained all this to her, 'if Primrose ducks another beach party that would be pretty serious, right?'

'It would be suicidal,' I said. 'Bianca would go mental.'

'The end of their friendship?'

'For sure. But Primrose wouldn't dare.'

Becky thought about this.

'What if she had a really big incentive?'

'Such as?'

'Such as thinking that Matt was going to be at the barbecue.'

'It doesn't look like he is,' I said.

'That doesn't matter,' said Becky. 'She just needs to think he's coming. Then she'll be desperate to get Bianca out of the way at the barbecue and she definitely won't want to leave early to go to the beach party.'

Becky said all I had to do was make Primrose think Matt was coming to the barbecue. How hard could that be? Ooh... it was a cunning plan! It couldn't possibly fail.

By the time I got home I was starting to have second thoughts. What if they rumbled me? I've never been the world's best liar. But the first thing I saw when I walked in was Bianca's weasely face, and I knew I had to go for it.

They were sitting round the kitchen table finishing lunch.

'Mum,' I said, taking a handful of leftover crisps. 'Becky's invited Matt from the kennels to the barbecue tonight. Is that all right?'

'Of course, darling,' said Mum.

Mission accomplished, I got out of there quick-smart before I could start to look shifty. I went to my room, leaving the door open so I'd be able to hear what happened next.

The plan worked like a dream. I would have texted Becky, only I couldn't find my phone. First Primrose tried the not-feeling-well thing but Bianca laughed it off.

'We only have to stay at the barbecue for an hour, and after that we're going to the party even if I have to carry you down there on my back!'

Then Primrose tried the family-stuff-is-just-so-boring approach.

'You don't have to come to the barbecue,' she told Bianca. 'It's going to be such a yawn! You could go straight to the beach and I'll meet you down there as soon as I can get away.'

All afternoon, Primrose wriggled like a worm on a hook but Bianca wouldn't let her off. They were going to the barbecue and then they were going to the beach party, end of.

By five o'clock time was running out. Mum was next door helping to organise the food and Dad was firing up the barbecue. Whoever put him in charge needed their head tested after the last time.

Primrose and Bianca came upstairs to her room to get ready. I thought Primrose must have given up trying to get rid of Bianca, but while Bianca was washing her hair in the bathroom Primrose ran noisily down the stairs and out the back door.

I peeped out the window and saw her striding up and down in the yard. What was she up to? After a few minutes she came back inside and ran back up the stairs, just in time to bump into Bianca on the landing with a towel wrapped round her head.

'Honestly!' Primrose gasped. 'You won't believe it! Mum and Dad have just told me I can't go to the lifeguards' party. It's so unfair!'

Bianca didn't say anything. I could hear every word but I couldn't see their faces. I crept towards the door but I couldn't quite bring myself to put my eye up to the gap.

'Well, I told them,' Primrose carried on, 'if you stop me going to the party then you needn't think I'll come to Mr Kaminski's barbecue!'

Quiet again. Total silence.

Primrose said, 'S-so I'm g-going to stay in my room and have an early night. S-serve them right, yeah?'

I heard Bianca take a deep breath.

'Are you giving me the brush-off?'

Primrose left a fatal pause. Bianca dived straight into it.

'You are! You're trying to get rid of me! You ungrateful little toad!'

She went off like a rocket, shouting and swearing at Primrose, calling her all sorts of names.

'I'm sorry, I'm so sorry,' Primrose kept saying. Then she poured fuel on the fire. 'It's just tonight. It's just one beach party.'

'One beach party?' cried Bianca. 'Last time was one beach party. This makes two beach parties and that's two too many!'

Primrose tried to say something but Bianca wasn't having any of it.

'You needn't think I'm going to stick up for you at school any more. Wait till I tell everyone what a snivelling little kid you are!' She put on a high whiny voice. 'Mummy and Daddy won't let me go to the party, boo hoo!'

Primrose made a sort of strangled gasp. She dived into the bathroom and locked the door. I didn't blame her. Part of me wanted to stay out of sight as well. But I was fed up of hiding from Bianca in my own house. I stepped boldly out onto the landing.

Bianca was standing there in a bath-towel like an exploding beetroot, bright red and fit to burst.

'I might have known you'd be there, ear-wigging as usual!' she yelled.

She started to storm out but then realised she didn't have any clothes on. Swear word, swear word, swear word, swear word, swear word! Back into Primrose's bedroom she went, flinging things off the bed, trying to find her clothes.

'Get lost!' she cried, kicking the door shut in my face.

A few minutes later, after a lot of crashing and muttering, she flung the door open again. Her hair looked like a pile of knotted knitting slipping down the side of her head and she had her top on back-to-front. She still couldn't storm out because she couldn't find her shoes.

'They're in the sitting room,' I said. 'Mind you don't slip on the stairs!'

Bianca pushed past me. She marched down to the sitting room and came straight out again with her shoes in her hand.

'Bye-bye, Bianca!'

Bang, bang, bang, she stamped down the last flight of stairs to the kitchen. Crash! She slammed the front door behind her.

Primrose came out of the bathroom. She was shaking like she'd just got off the fastest ride in the fun-park. She collapsed into her bedroom and shut the door. She was either going to get changed for the barbecue or dive under the duvet – it could go either way.

I went back into my bedroom and looked out the window. The guests were beginning to arrive. Mum was moving among them pouring drinks and Dad was already busy burning things on the barbecue. I got changed and brushed my hair, ready to go down and join in.

The doorbell rang. I bumped into Primrose coming out of her room. She had put on some make-up but I could tell that she'd been crying.

'It'll be Becky,' I said.

She followed me down the stairs and as I went to open the front door she slipped out the back so as to be ready to meet Becky and, as she thought, Matt at the barbecue.

'It worked, then!' said Becky, grinning from ear to ear. 'I just passed Bianca steaming down the path with a face like a slapped haddock!'

I tried to look pleased but I was beginning to wish we hadn't played such a mean trick on Primrose. First she had faced up to Bianca and then she had somehow managed to pick herself up and pull herself together ready to meet the boy of her dreams... when all the time we knew he wasn't coming.

'Tell me what happened,' Becky said. 'I want all the details!'

But I had only just begun when a loud cheery voice came wafting up the hill towards us.

'Hi, Becky! Hi, Peony!'

Matt was striding up the zig-zag path. I shut my eyes but when I opened them again he was still there.

'I've brought your phone,' he said, taking the steps two at a time. 'You left it on the counter at lunchtime.'

'Oh... well... thank you!'

Becky and I exchanged a look. Could it be that we might get Matt to the barbecue after all? The words 'icing' and 'cake' came to mind!

'Have you finished the fencing?' Becky asked. 'Can you come to the barbecue after all?'

'We-ell...' goes Matt.

Me and Becky grabbed an arm each and started pulling him inside. He laughed and pretended to struggle. We were larking around on the doorstep when he suddenly stopped.

'Something's on fire!' he yelled. I looked behind me. Outside the back windows the yard was filling up with smoke.

'Don't worry, that's just – ' I started, but Matt pushed past me, grabbed the fire extinguisher from the hook near the cooker and ran outside. Becky and me ran out after him.

From somewhere above the smoke zone we heard Dad's voice.

'The sausages are done!'

'That's what I was trying to tell you,' I said to Matt. 'It's just my dad doing a barbecue. Last time, somebody actually called the fire brigade.'

Matt put the fire extinguisher down. Mum appeared on the other side of the fence. 'Is that you, Peony?' She flapped her hands to clear the smoke away. 'Oh, and this must be Becky and Matt from the kennels. Hello!'

I had forgotten that Primrose wasn't the only one who thought Matt was coming – so did Mum. She told him and Becky to climb over the fence and come and get a drink.

Matt hesitated. He probably realised that if he stepped over that fence, sooner or later he would be obliged to eat a lump of charcoal which had once been a sausage stuffed into a hot dog roll.

'Come!' cried Mr Kaminski, seeing us hovering. He reached over and shook Matt's hand. 'You friend of Pinker family, yes? They lovely people. They give me this cardigan! You like?' He more or less pulled Matt over the fence. Then he offered Becky his hand, like an old-fashioned gentleman, and Matt joined in, offering me his. He had clearly decided the situation was funny and was starting to enjoy himself.

We went to get a drink and there, behind the fruit punch and jugs of lemonade, was Primrose. She looked as if she could either fall apart or do a runner at any moment.

'This is my sister, Primrose,' I said quickly, before she had a chance to bolt.

Matt offered her his hand.

'What a lovely name!' he said.

Chapter 17

Dad in the shed, not hiding from the dog, and the return of the Pekinese

Dad was in an exceptionally good mood at Mr Kaminski's barbecue, even better than usual when he's outside burning burgers and scorching sausages.

'It's been a good-news, bad-news kind of day,' he said, 'and the good news won!'

The bad news was that Daphne had phoned Ed to tell him she was never coming back. She had fallen in love with her water-skiing instructor.

'The good news is... I was right!' Dad said. 'There *were* plenty more fish in the sea!'

The bad news was that Ed wanted Dad to take over the problem page permanently since he finally seemed to have got the hang of it.

'The good news is... Mr Kaminski has agreed to do it for me!'

Mr Kaminski grinned and nodded. He looked bright and happy in his brand new cardigan, not at all like a sad old snail any more.

Mum was also in an exceptionally good mood because everyone kept saying what a great job she had done on his garden. Lots of people asked if she would come and sort out their gardens for them.

Mum said maybe she and Stella should think about starting up their own gardening business.

'We could call it Garden Angels,' she said.

'That's a brilliant idea,' goes Stella. 'Then I can tell that plant-poisoner Price what he can do with his job!'

Primrose was in an ecstatic mood because of Matt. Obviously, me and Becky didn't crowd them or anything, but we couldn't help sometimes overhearing what they were talking about. It was slow going at first – I mean, all they really had in common was me.

'Peony's a great kid, isn't she?' goes Matt.

'She's lovely,' Primrose agreed, mushily.

'Ma says she works really hard with the dogs. She's dog-crazy, that girl!'

'Yes,' said Primrose. 'It's such a pity for Peony that we can't ever have one of our own.'

She explained about Dad being scared of dogs, and about her plan to try and help him get over it by visiting the un-scary dogs at the kennels, such as old Sam. She didn't mention the fact that she'd had an ulterior motive, of course.

'If your dad won't come to the kennels,' said Matt, 'maybe I could bring Sam to your house some time.'

'That's a brilliant idea!' goes Primrose. 'How about tomorrow?'

'I'm at the cafe tomorrow...'

'When you've finished work, then? We could hang around here for a bit and then maybe take Sam for a walk on the cliff path.'

So now they had a shared project – getting a dog for me! – and they'd also fixed up their first date.

All day Sunday, Primrose was on her mobile sending messages, pics and texts to Matt. She spent about a billion hours trying to make up her mind what to wear. By the time he arrived her whole bed had disappeared under a mountain of clothes she had tried on and rejected.

I don't know how the rest of the date went but the getting-Dad-used-to-dogs-by-bringing-friendly-old-Sam-round could definitely have gone better. When Matt and Sam arrived, Dad was sitting on the bottom step oiling the squeaky wheel of the wheelbarrow. The minute he clapped eyes on Sam he leapt off the steps and dived into the shed.

'It's only Sam,' goes Matt. 'He's very old and not at all scary!'

'I'm not scared. I'm just looking for...' Dad scanned the inside of the shed but we don't keep anything in there except the wheelbarrow. '... for this lolly wrapper to wipe the spare oil off with!' He hung around under there like a mole in a hole until Matt and Sam had gone on up the steps and were safely in the house.

Matt and Primrose agreed they should not give up. If needs be, Matt said, he was prepared to bring old Sam up every day after school until Dad stopped being scared of him. Primrose somehow managed not to jump up and down for joy.

By the end of the weekend everything was looking good, but I couldn't help worrying about what might happen when Primrose went back to school. Supposing Bianca was really horrible to her... or even worse, supposing she decided to forgive her and be friends again?

It seemed a long way down the zig-zag path after school on Monday, not knowing what I would find when I got to the house. I couldn't quite bring myself to believe that Bianca had gone for good.

Well, you know when something bad has been happening every single day, such as your sister Primrose bringing her horrible new best friend home after school? On that Monday afternoon, it didn't!

I walked in to find Primrose making pancakes. There were two plates on the table, two half-lemons and a bowl of sugar... and Bianca was nowhere to be seen.

'Hurry up, Peony,' she said. 'This one's yours and it's ready.'

I dropped my bag on the floor and grabbed a plate. Primrose tossed the pancake up in the air and I lunged forward to catch it.

'How was school?' I said, as I drenched it in sugar and lemon.

'So-so,' shrugged Primrose, pouring another cup of batter into the pan.

She told me Bianca had been really mean to her all day, spreading nasty rumours and everything, but she didn't care – she was in love!

'I never really liked her, you know,' she said.

'Why were you friends with her, then?'

Primrose said the reason she'd wanted us to call her Annabel was because at that time she really did hate her name. All the kids at school had been teasing her about it. That was why she first got friendly with Bianca. 'No-one teases you when you're hanging out with someone like her.'

The trouble was, Bianca made her do all kinds of things she didn't want to, such as bunking off school and trying to get invited to the lifeguards' beach parties, and pretending to think they could be pop stars when she knew very well that neither of them could sing. Most of all, she didn't want to join in being horrible to me. She just kind of got sucked in, and then she couldn't get out again.

'Bianca isn't the kind of person you want to not be friends with,' she said.

I told her it seemed to me that if Bianca was a dog she would be a Pit Bull. Nobody gives you bother if you've got one of those by your side but the problem with having a fighting dog is it can turn against its owner.

Primrose nodded thoughtfully. 'That's an interesting way of looking at it,' she said.

She flipped her pancake onto a plate and poured

some more batter into the pan for me.

I said if Mum was a dog she'd be a Shetland sheepdog, quick and keen to work – if Dad was a dog he'd be a comfy old Labrador lolling on the settee.

'If I was a dog,' said Primrose, rolling her pancake up and chomping a bit off the end, 'what do you think I would be?'

'We-ell...'

'Go on – say it! I know you've thought of one.'

I had a feeling things might be about to go horribly wrong, but she did ask.

'Before you got snarly with Bianca, I always thought you would be a Pekinese.'

'A Pekinese?' goes Primrose. 'Why? What are they like?'

I told her they came from China and the legend said they were a cross between a lion and a monkey. I read that in the Bumper Book of Dogs.

'They're brave and bossy, that's the lion part,' I said. 'But they're also friendly and fun.'

Primrose laughed. 'Fair enough!' she said. 'What do they look like – more lion or more monkey?'

'They're kind of hard to describe.'

'Show me a picture, then.'

It was too late to get out of it so I went and got the Bumper Book of Dogs. I opened it at the right page and handed it to Primrose. I could see she wasn't impressed.

'What's that supposed to be?' she demanded. 'It looks like a cat that's crashed into a window!'

'I didn't say you *looked* like a Pekinese, Primrose...'

'Whatever!' she interrupted me. She didn't want us to fall out again so soon, but you could tell she was cross. 'I can't hang around here anyway! Matt's coming in half an hour and I don't know what I'm going to wear.'

With that, she flounced off, leaving me to clear up the mess and wash the dishes. I grinned to myself. That was a Pekinese for you – sometimes amazing and sometimes annoying. It was good to have the old Primrose back.

Will Peony get a dog? Will Primrose and Matt live happily ever after? Find out what happens next in

How to Get the Family You Want
by Peony Pinker.

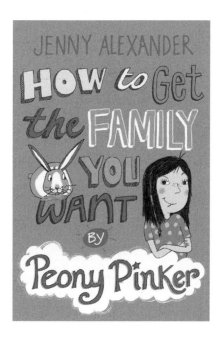